THE MARVELOUS
MISADVENTURES OF
SEBASTIAN

THE MARVELOUS MISADVENTURES OF SEBASTIAN

Grand Extravaganza, Including
a Performance by the Entire Cast of
the Gallimaufry-Theatricus

by LLOYD ALEXANDER

A Yearling Book

Published by
Dell Publishing
a division of
Bantam Doubleday Dell Publishing Group, Inc.
666 Fifth Avenue
New York, New York 10103

The trademark Yearling® is registered in the U.S. Patent and
Trademark Office.

The trademark Dell® is registered in the U.S. Patent and
Trademark Office.

ISBN: 0-440-40549-1

Reprinted by arrangement with E. P. Dutton

Printed in the United States of America

December 1991

10 9 8 7 6 5 4 3 2 1

OPM

For willing listeners ॐ

CONTENTS ❦

Contents

THE MARVELOUS
MISADVENTURES OF
SEBASTIAN

I ✤ How Sebastian Lost His Place

From his perch on the window ledge of the musicians' quarters, high under the East Wing roof, Sebastian's quick ears caught the drum of hoofbeats. In another moment, he spied a coach-and-four galloping through the gates, down the tree-shaded avenue, past the swans in the pool, to rein up at the Grand Hall of the Baron's estate. Two footmen leaped off, flung open the coach door, and with much effort handed out a gross, waddling figure in a gold-braided cocked hat and scarlet cloak. At first sight of the unexpected visitor, Sebastian tumbled back into the chamber and shouted a warning:

"The Purse!"

The Second and Third Fiddles and a Flute were playing cards, while the aged and ailing First Fiddle lay stretched on his bed. Hearing Sebastian's alarm, the Flute bolted out the door and the others hurriedly struggled into their livery. Bells began shrilling on every floor of every wing, alerting all the household to this visitation from Count Lobelieze, Royal Treasurer and First Minister of Finance—whom Sebastian preferred to call by a less dignified title.

The First Fiddle started up. His cheeks twitched with fright. Though he had served the Baron longer than any-one on the estate, the old musician had gone practically deaf and lived in constant terror of being found out.

"Sebastian!" he moaned. "Friend and colleague! Ah, my boy, my boy, what shall I do? Today of all days, if I miss a note it will be worth my skin!"

Sebastian clapped him on the shoulder. "What shall you do? Why, just what we did last time His Tub-of-Lardship came to squeeze gold from the Baron. You pretend to play, and make a show of leading us. I'll play your part easily enough. The Baron will be none the wiser. As for The Purse—His Most Excellent Haunch-and-Paunch hears nothing past the rumbling of his own stomach."

Glad to help the pitiful First Fiddle, and by no means unwilling to pull off a harmless hoodwinking, Sebastian jumped into his livery, snatched up his fiddle and bow, and raced down the stairs.

There he saw that his master, Baron Purn-Hessel, had been caught as unawares as the rest of the household. The Baron's wig was askew, his neckcloth was hastily tied, and a pair of reading spectacles hung from his pocket.

"An honor," murmured the Baron, a sickly smile frozen on his face as he escorted the Royal Treasurer into the Grand Hall. "Honor, indeed . . . your coming this far from Loringhold. All goes well in the capital? The Regent's health excellent? And yours? Splendid as al-ways?"

The Purse, monstrously fat, with great slabs of jowls and a mouth as wide as a toad's, heaved along beside the

Baron. His gold waistcoat, bulging with watches and snuffboxes, scarcely covered his paunch; a thickly powdered wig crouched on top of his head; his white breeches were stretched tight to bursting; and his boots creaked under his tread. He stared at his anxious host through liverish eyes, choosing to disregard the Baron's remarks in favor of his own.

"An event of greatest magnitude," The Purse declared. "An occasion of utmost importance to the entire Principality of Hamelin-Loring. You will be pleased to learn the Regent intends to announce the betrothal of Princess Isabel."

Baron Purn-Hessel bobbed his head. "Betrothal—of utmost importance, quite so. Princess Isabel's betrothal to—?"

"To the Regent himself, naturally," replied The Purse. "Beyond question, the only appropriate union. Your official notification will arrive in due course. Meanwhile, the Regent allows you the privilege of offering, shall we say, a personal gift—in addition to the customary tokens of esteem. You know the Regent's thoughtfulness, and he is sensible it may take longer than usual, even for one in your position, to arrange a sum befitting the occasion." The Purse smiled at the Baron and added, "In gold crowns, if you please. Without undue delay."

"Princess Isabel to wed—the Regent?" Baron Purn-Hessel answered weakly. "My heartiest congratulations to the happy couple. By all means assure the Regent: without undue delay. Gold crowns, of course."

The Baron's voice faltered, though he tried to keep his composure by adding, with hollow enthusiasm, "Now, sir, you've traveled far and no doubt have many more visits

to make. But if you would favor us with your company
. . . a small repast . . . a little music."

The Purse grimaced at this last. Seeing the Royal
Treasurer's disdain, Baron Purn-Hessel winced. Like all
the nobility and gentry in Hamelin-Loring, the Baron
spared no pains in catering to any whim of the Regent's
creature. The Principality was not so large that unfavora-
ble reports did not reach the Glorietta Palace in Loringhold with distressing speed; and even from a distance, the
all-powerful Regent, Count Grinssorg, could repay a
slight misjudgment with sudden ruin.

Sebastian, overhearing all this, pulled a wry face,
knowing as well as any in the household that after The
Purse's visit there would be lean fare at the Baron's table
and leaner fare at the servants' board. Baron Purn-Hessel
was not a cheeseparing master, but the Regent's new demand would leave little cheese to pare.

Joining the dozen musicians behind their stands, Sebastian tucked his fiddle under his chin and began tun-
ing the strings. The Baroness with her two small
daughters, all gowned alike in red silk, were making
their way down the marble staircase. Behind them followed the Maids of the Chamber, the Hairdresser, the
Dancing Master, and half-a-dozen lackeys hastily com-
mandeered as a joyous crowd to wait on The Purse's
pleasure. Baron Purn-Hessel glanced around to make
certain all was in order.

From his chair in the front rank of the orchestra, the
First Fiddle signaled the musicians to begin. The Purse,
meanwhile, raised the outstretched hand of the Baroness
to his lips, put one fat leg behind him, and bent as
deeply as he could.

At the same instant, Sebastian lifted his bow to launch into the opening notes. As he did, the fiddle head hit the music stand. His hand faltered and the bow went skidding up the strings, sounding like the rasp of cloth tearing down the middle.

The Purse straightened as if stabbed. He flung away the hand of the Baroness while his own sped to the seat of his breeches which, from the sound, had surely split in two.

The Baron paled. The Grand Hall fell utterly silent. The lackeys stood stiff as dead men. The Baroness did not blink an eye; but the two little girls crammed their fists into their mouths and tried vainly to stifle their giggling.

Finding his breeches safe, The Purse realized the embarrassing noise had come from one of the musicians. He went crimson and livid by turns. His hands clenched, his waistcoat stretched even tighter, his jowls shook and swelled all the more, and he burst out in a furious voice:

"Who did that?"

The glare of The Purse fell on the nearest musician, the First Fiddle, who began trembling violently, gasping, and looking ready to topple from his chair.

Sebastian, at first scarcely able to hold back his laughter, now understood that serious damage had been done: not to The Purse's breeches but to The Purse's dignity. Seeing that the courtier's wrath would surely fall on the wretched First Fiddle, who seemed about to shatter into pieces at any moment, Sebastian quickly stepped forward, and bowed to Count Lobelieze.

"Excellency, it was I. My bow slipped."

The Purse stared at him as at a slug on a dinner plate.

"Impudent villain! You dare look me in the eye? And lie to my face? Well, young scoundrel, I'll have the truth out of you! Admit it! You did it on purpose to mock your betters!"

"Excellency," Sebastian declared, "you have my word: an accident, no more than that."

"What!" roared The Purse, turning to Baron Purn-Hessel. "Do you hear him? He raises his eyes, and now his voice! Rebellion! No more, no less! But he'll be taken down, sir, for I know how to deal with his kind."

The Baron gave Sebastian a reassuring glance, and raised a hand placatingly to The Purse. "Surely, Count, it must be as he says. I know him for something of a scamp, but there's no harm in him."

"No harm in him?" retorted The Purse. "Do you call disrespect and insolence no harm? Will you have all your household follow his example? Ah, no, sir!" He turned to Sebastian. "You'll beg my forgiveness. On your knees, you villain!"

Sebastian flushed. "Excellency," he said, looking squarely at The Purse, "I'll stand like a man and ask your pardon for my clumsiness. I'd not be such a fool as to offend Your Excellency on purpose. Though indeed I'd be more than a fool and less than a man if I admitted something I never meant."

This only sent The Purse into greater fury. "More insolence! Impudence on top of impudence! Purn-Hessel, I'll tolerate no more!"

"He will be soundly punished," the Baron murmured.

"He will be dismissed! Discharged! At once!" The Purse bellowed. "Let him be gone this instant!"

The Baron hesitated. "Count Lobelieze—I should hate to lose such a nimble fiddler."

The Purse went closer to him and muttered between his teeth:

"Tell me nothing of fiddlers! Have you crowns enough to waste on a worthless musician? A rebel and renegade, to boot! The Regent tolerates neither, and he will be curious to learn that you do."

At this mention of the Regent, Baron Purn-Hessel went even paler and his eyes wavered. He said nothing for a moment. The Purse folded his arms.

The Baron finally turned helplessly to Sebastian and spoke in a low, pained voice:

"You are dismissed. Leave here directly. You no longer have a place in my service."

Sebastian gave his master a puzzled glance; but when the Baron said no more, he bowed stiffly, turned on his heel, and marched from the Grand Hall.

He made his way to the East Wing and up the stairs to the musicians' quarters, his dismay, confusion, and indignation growing at every step, and his blood boiling at the loathsome Purse. "I'm in for it this time," he groaned.

Nevertheless, he could not seriously believe the Baron meant to turn him out. "When I galloped his favorite mare across the swan pool he only stopped my pocket money for a fortnight," he told himself. "Even when I bloodied the Second Footman's nose for teasing the Scullery Maid, and ruined his livery into the bargain—the Baron did nothing at all."

Still, much as he expected it, no servant came to tell him the Baron had changed his mind. More than ever baffled and for the first time truly alarmed, Sebastian could only do as he had been ordered.

Though he delayed as long as he dared, it took him little time to pack. The livery was not his to keep, and his other belongings were scant: jacket and breeches, a few changes of linen, a couple of shirts, one pair of boots, two pairs of stockings, and a neckerchief. He dressed slowly, then wrapped the remaining garments around his only other possessions—his fiddle and bow—and tucked them all into a green bag.

It was in his mind that Baron Purn-Hessel would call him back before he reached the gate; but as he passed through the kitchen, not even a lackey whispered a word to him. The Chief Cook, who had always spared some tasty morsel for him, bit his lips and kept busy over the pots and pans. The First Footman, who had always winked at his escapades, now stared, speechless. The Serving Maids, all of whom at one time or another had sworn him undying love, turned their eyes tearfully away.

Sebastian, as much distressed by their silence as by his own plight, soon saw the reason for it. Two of The Purse's footmen, a pair of grim-faced fellows, were lounging at a table in the corner, keeping a sharp eye on all that happened. Sebastian made his way from the kitchen without a word.

The Gatekeeper alone dared to offer a leave-taking, but only after the iron gates of Baron Purn-Hessel's estate clanged shut and the old servant was sure of not being overheard.

"Farewell, and have a care," murmured the Gatekeeper, thrusting his hand between the bars. "It's a hard piece of business, the world; alas, you'll need more than that yellow hair and handsome face of yours. Mind your steps, lad, or you'll be for prison—or worse."

"Prison?" Sebastian replied, putting as light a face on the matter as he could. "Why, it seems to me I'm on the free side of the gate!"

The Gatekeeper sadly shook his head. "Locked in and bolted more than any of us here." He pointed with his keys toward the road. "Locked into the *outside*, if you take my meaning."

At that, he shuffled into his gatehouse, leaving Sebastian with no more to do than set off wherever he chose.

BEWILDERED at the harshness of his punishment, angry at being humbled by a hog's head like The Purse, and fearful of what lay in store for him now, Sebastian trudged along as his legs led him. Even so, at each step, he could not help glancing over his shoulder, hoping to see one of the stable boys come galloping up, shouting that the Baron had ordered his return. But the road lay empty behind him; and though he slowed to a snail's pace, the Purn-Hessel estate was all too soon out of sight. His feet were leading him nowhere, and he knew only one thing for certain: his hope for a living lay in the bag on his back.

Nevertheless, the Baron had called him a nimble fiddler, and the more Sebastian thought of this, the more his spirits lifted.

"So be it," he told himself. "I've lost my place, but I'm bound to find another. And who's to say it won't be even better?" He remembered the Second Fiddle once saying that New Locking, though small, was proud of its village band and paid its musicians well. The Flute always claimed that the most openhanded master was old Count

Benda, who kept a fine estate near the busy town of
Darmstel. Spire, however, had an excellent opera house
and theatre, and was also the closest. Loringhold was farthest, but this greatest city of the realm might offer the
best fortune of all.

At this, his imagination kindled, and his steps caught
the rhythm as he repeated: "Darmstel or Loringhold?
New Locking? Spire?" And soon he began striding along
more hopefully, kicking a pebble in front of him, and
making a game of keeping it moving without missing a
beat. The towns, as he named them, danced through his
mind. Glittering with promise, each beckoned so win-
ningly he could not choose among them, and he began
feeling certain beyond question of finding the finest place
in Hamelin-Loring.

By late afternoon, however, he was too footsore,
thirsty, and hungry to imagine anything more splendid
than a hot meal and a soft bed. And so he was happy
when finally he arrived at a lopsided cluster of timber-
and-plaster houses with thatched roofs. A handful of
idlers joked among themselves in front of the smithy. In
the middle of the market square, a stone trough served as
both town fountain and horse pond.

But he noticed, above the courtyard gate of one building, a wooden signboard lettered "The Merry Host of
Dorn." Though its colors had weathered badly, Sebastian
made out the painting of a hearty, apple-cheeked face
grinning broadly, with one eye shut in a jolly wink.
Cheered by such happy promise of warm welcome, he
hurried across the square to the door of the inn and
lifted the latch.

In the low-ceilinged eating room, travelers of all sorts

crowded the plank tables: peddlers with their packs; vegetable growers on the way home from market; a number of drovers, big, good-natured-looking men who had brought their cattle from the outlying farms to sell at Dorn. Sebastian's mouth watered as he spied the joint of beef sizzling on a spit in the great fireplace. A spotted dog, harnessed to a treadmill turning the spit, yelped pitifully after a lure of meat hung just beyond his nose; and whenever the creature showed signs of wearying, a greasy-fingered potboy prodded his lean ribs with a wooden spoon.

"Poor dog," Sebastian thought. "His belly must be even emptier than mine."

He glanced around for the innkeeper, expecting to recognize him easily from the portrait on the signboard. Instead, he saw a gaunt, stoop-shouldered man in a soiled apron, a dour, scowling fellow with a sharp jaw and hard, close-set eyes. Nevertheless, Sebastian stepped up to the self-styled Merry Host, bowed courteously, and said:

"Friend, your house looks pleasanter to me every minute. I'm on my way to Spire, but I'll gladly break my journey here and stay the night, for I've walked my legs off down to my knees. If I'm too early for supper, whatever's ready in your kitchen will do very well. I'm hungry enough to swallow the pots and pans, along with anything that's in them!"

Through all this, the Merry Host had been eyeing Sebastian from the top of his hatless head to the toes of his scuffed boots. Instead of rousing the potboy and leading Sebastian to a table, he bent forward and said in a sour voice:

"Show me your money."

"Why, friend," Sebastian replied, "do you take me for a vagabond? I'm a fiddler, and might well be a First Fiddle before all's said and done." He pulled out the handful of coins from his pocket. "Now then, to meat! And I'll trust you to charge me no more than what's fair."

The Merry Host stared at his would-be guest in amazement, having seen all he needed of the coppers in Sebastian's hand.

"Do you take me for an idiot?" cried the innkeeper. "Are you a fool? A knave? Or both? To call for beef and bed when you've not enough for a bale of hay in my stable! First Fiddle? First Booby! This is the world, my fine fiddler, not Cloud-Cuckoo Land! When you know the price of what you want, and can pay it, come back. Meantime, be off!"

Sebastian was startled and more than put down by the innkeeper's outburst. Serving Baron Purn-Hessel, he had never concerned himself with the price of beef and bed, let alone a bale of hay; and it had never come into his head to count the money in his pocket. Crestfallen and confused, he was about to turn away when a sudden thought made him call to the innkeeper:

"Wait! I'll strike a bargain with you."

"You'll strike no bargain with me," snapped the Merry Host, "unless you've struck gold in the past minute."

"That I have," Sebastian said, "and so have you." He untied his green bag and drew out his fiddle.

Seeing it, the Merry Host impatiently shook his head. "I buy no fiddles here."

"Nor do I sell mine," Sebastian returned. "But I'll sell you some tunes from it, and entertain your company."

"Meat, not music, is their cheer," said the Merry Host.

"And the only tune I care to hear is a ducat ringing in my till."

"You'll hear better than a ducat, I promise you," Sebastian went on quickly. "A lively air puts everyone in good spirits. Your customers will stay to sing and dance. The more they sing, the drier for your drink; and the more they dance, the hungrier for your food."

The Merry Host scratched his chin and pondered a while. "The scrape of your fiddle for a slice of my meat? No. And yet—it might prove a fair exchange."

"A bargain, then!" Sebastian cried. "Now, to supper! I could eat that joint, bone, gristle, and all."

"Not so fast," said the Merry Host. "You'll have my fare after I've had your fiddling. And I'll tell you this, my lad: How you fill your belly hangs on how you fill my cashbox."

Grudgingly, the Merry Host gave Sebastian leave to put his bag in the stable and wash himself at the innyard pump. The prospect of the feast awaiting him added zest to Sebastian's appetite.

"My fiddle's my living, no mistake about it," he said to himself, "and better than I thought, if it can play me a supper from that sour-tempered, flint-skinned Merry Host, who doesn't look as if he fattens himself on his own fare!"

Clasping the fiddle in his arms, he danced like a grasshopper across the cobbled yard. Before he reached the pump, however, he heard rough voices shouting:

"Burned alive, I say! Green wood and a slow fire!"

"No! Flogged first! I'll have his skin, if no other parts of him!"

The clamor came from the middle of the innyard,

where a few of the drovers had joined the townsmen and idlers from the smithy. The voices grew louder, mingling with hoots and laughter. Craning his neck, Sebastian glimpsed a net swinging from a rope at the end of a pole. What the snare held he could not make out, but it thrashed wildly. He edged his way through the crowd.

Slipping past one of the townsmen standing with hands on hips and gawking at the sight, Sebastian stopped short. His eyes widened and he gasped aloud. Two men, the first a burly fellow and the second thin as a ferret with a broad-brimmed hat on the back of his head, scuffled to wrench the pole from each other's grip, while their friends shouted, laughed, and egged them on. In the net was a cat.

Foul with mire, blood-spattered, one ear torn, the cat hissed, spat furiously, and flung itself against the net, screaming and thrusting its claws through the mesh as if it meant to repay its abusers even at the cost of its own life.

"What's this?" cried Sebastian. "What are you doing to that poor cat?"

At Sebastian's outburst, the two men stopped and gaped at him. One of their comrades raised a heavy hand to push Sebastian aside, saying:

"Mind your tongue! Keep your nose out of our business!"

"We spent days to trap the villain," put in another. "But we've got him now, and there's an end to our troubles. Right, Skimmerhorn?"

"Yes, and the start of his," declared the burly man who had been thus addressed. He thrust his face as close to the net as he dared, while the cat snarled in rage. "Hear me? What do you say to that? Speak up, curse you! Oh, you'll sing well enough before we're done with you."

"Let him taste my whip first," cried the ferretlike man. "He'll soon find his voice."

Sebastian stared around him. "Are the folk of Dorn all madmen? Torture a cat to make him speak? "

"Cat?" cried Skimmerhorn. "You're a bigger fool than you look. That's no cat! The vile brute's a witch!"

𝒜 witch?" Sebastian said, taken aback for an instant. The animal stopped struggling and turned its head to watch him steadily with bright blue eyes. Its mouth opened in a soundless cry. Sebastian went closer. "The poor creature has a tail exactly like a cat, and ears and whiskers like one. Indeed, friend, I'd have to say he's every bit of a cat, and not a witch at all."

"The more fool you," snapped the ferrety man, whose name was Spargel. "A witch takes any shape."

"If that's true, this one's made a poor choice," replied Sebastian. "Have a care, then, for he may turn into a griffin and gobble you up."

Spargel drew back uneasily, but Skimmerhorn took a closer grip on the pole and declared:

"He'll not change his shape. A black cat is what all witches and wizards favor. That's why he's turned himself into one."

"A black cat?" Sebastian repeated. "If you don't count the dirt, he looks altogether white to me."

"Yes, and there's the slyness of him," said Spargel. "To

show himself white and put honest folk off their guard. But you can be sure, secretly he's black as pitch."

"That's common sense," a townsman agreed, solemnly nodding his head. "If it was me who was a black witch-cat, I'd let none find out. But for all his cunning, he's given himself away. I've seen gray-striped, mustard, and piebald cats, but never a white, blue-eyed one like this. Unnatural, that's what he is, as any fool can see."

"If he was blue, yellow, or speckled green, he'd not escape us," said the burly Skimmerhorn. "He should burn for his oddness if nothing else. But his deeds show his devil's nature. He's done what only a witch can do."

"What now," Sebastian said, "since he's a black cat in the guise of a white cat, you'll tell me he proves his witchcraft by opposites? By not flying through the air? By not riding a broomstick? By not casting spells?"

"Do you make sport of us?" cried a snaggle-toothed townsman in a grimy jacket. "Do you throw dust in our eyes with your talk? You've a clever tongue, but we know what we know. There's been spells cast a-plenty, and only bad luck since we caught sight of him in Dorn."

"It was I saw him first," boasted Skimmerhorn. "You can thank me for smelling him out. I glimpsed him in the bushes by Mistress Irma's cottage, the very day I made up my mind to court her. But she threw a jug at my head. Oh, I knew then some fiend must have bewitched her. And sure enough, there the beast was, crouching in the turnips, staring and mocking me with a witchy grin. I saw him then for what he is."

"I too," Spargel joined in. "Coming home from the Merry Host one midnight, a dizziness took me so I could hardly keep my feet. Next thing I knew, there was I, flat on my back looking up at the moon. And not a penny in my pocket, though I had a ducat when I left. It was the cat to blame! He crossed my path just before I fell. Made me stumble on his shadow! Then sneaked back and robbed my pockets, to boot!"

"Since he's come to Dorn," Skimmerhorn added, "there's been rainstorms, hailstorms, frogs in the ditches, weeds in the gardens, and not one good thing happen to any of us. You wanted proof? There you have it."

"Friends, friends," cried Sebastian, "can't you see that you've blamed a wretched stray cat when there's none to blame but yourselves and the weather? There's no fairness in that, and no witch in your net."

Skimmerhorn's face took on an ugly scowl. "The more you take his part, the more I wonder if you're in league with him."

"Have a care," Spargel added. "He's had his trial. Yours may be next."

"Trial?" retorted Sebastian, whose blood had begun to boil at Spargel's threat. "A court where you're witnesses and judges both?" He stepped closer. "Well, I'll give you my oath: I'll not stand by and let a helpless thing suffer. Since the cat can't testify, I'll do it for him and say this much: Let him go, or you'll have a hard case to settle with me."

"We'll deal with you," declared Spargel, "after the witch is flogged to death."

"Burned, I tell you!" cried Skimmerhorn, and the pair began fighting again.

"Neither!" one of the drovers called out. "If that was the Regent at the end of your pole, I'd be your man. But the lad's right. It's only a harmless cat."

The snaggle-toothed man now chose to take a further hand in the matter. "Witch or not, we'll have our sport with the dirty beast."

"Sport?" returned the drover. "If it's sport you want, let's see if your arms are any stronger than your wits."

"So you shall," cried the other, letting fly with a blow to the drover's head. But the stout drover warded it off, seized the man around the middle, and heaved him into the crowd, setting the bystanders tumbling like ninepins.

Before Sebastian could join his unexpected ally, two of the townsman's cronies leaped against the drover, whose own comrades hurried to help him. In another instant, all were scuffling, yelling, cursing, and shoving back and forth in such confusion that no one could tell friend from foe.

A cobblestone skimmed past Sebastian's ear by a hairsbreadth and hit a window of the inn. The glass shattered with a great crash, and out burst the Merry Host with half a dozen of the company, bawling furiously.

Skimmerhorn had let fall the pole and was busy trading blows with Spargel. Sebastian dropped to hands and knees, and, while the fracas boiled above his head, he snatched up the net and hastily untied the rope. The cat shot out of the snare and went streaking through the tangle of legs.

Sebastian regained his feet; but as he did, a hard fist caught him squarely on the nose, setting off more fireworks in his head than ever he had seen at Baron Purn-Hessel's birthday celebrations. He sat down abruptly on the cobbles. Meantime, the witch-trappers, realizing their victim had escaped, swarmed out of the innyard, leaving behind only the Merry Host, who shook Sebastian unmercifully and shouted at the top of his voice:

"Brawler! Troublemaker! I knew you for a ne'er-do-well the moment I laid eyes on you!"

Sebastian sat up and held his head, which felt twice its size and weight and ready to fall off his shoulders at any moment. His jacket and shirt were soaked and clammy. Cautiously, he brought his fingers to his throbbing nose that seemed to have swollen even bigger than his head. He climbed unsteadily to his feet while the Merry Host roared in his ear:

"Smashed my window! Spoiled my trade! The turnspit dog run off and my best meat burned to a crisp!"

As Sebastian's eyes cleared, he caught sight of his green bag lying on the cobbles. Heedless of his bleeding nose and whirling head, he ran and snatched it up.

Fingers trembling, Sebastian untied the knot and reached in. The bow was undamaged, but the front and back of the fiddle were in splinters.

He stared at the wreckage and gasped, "My fiddle . . . my living. . . ."

"You're well paid for the mischief you've done," the innkeeper said coldly. "Just what you deserve."

Stunned, Sebastian dropped the fragments into the bag. Too dismayed to protest or explain, he could only stare blankly.

"Now," said the Merry Host, "I daresay you're brazen enough to ask for your supper. Well, put that notion straight out of your head. You're the one who struck the bargain with me. Ducats in my till? You've taken ducats out of my pocket, for all it will cost me to mend your damage. You're lucky I'm not thrashing the price of a window out of your skin. No, I'll count it a good lesson for me not to be so kindhearted and openhanded with brawlers and vagabonds."

The Merry Host laughed sourly. "Play for your supper, will you? I'd like to see you do it on that handful of kindling. Be off, or I'll have the constable toss you into the lock-up. Quick march! We don't welcome troublemakers in Dorn!"

IV ⤷ How Sebastian
Found a Friend

THE prospect of being thrown into jail, on top of all his other griefs, shook Sebastian from his daze. Clutching his bag under one arm and mopping his bleeding nose with his jacket sleeve, he set off as fast as his legs would carry him. He left the road at the first open field he came to, and cut across it until he could not be seen easily, fearful the witch-trappers might still be seeking their victim.

"And from what I've seen of Skimmerhorn and Spargel," he told himself, "they'd be just as happy to have me in their net."

At last, too weary to go farther, he sat down by a thicket near a stream and drew out the shattered fiddle to examine it more closely, hoping the damage was not quite as bad as it first had seemed. But the fiddle was indeed beyond repair. Sebastian shook his head.

"Well, there goes Spire—and Darmstel, New Locking, and Loringhold," he sighed, tossing the useless instrument into the bushes.

He turned away, then looked back in surprise. A pair of blue eyes was watching him from the thicket.

In another moment, the white cat picked its way out of the underbrush and padded toward him.

"Aha, so it's you," Sebastian said, brightening a little. He held out his hands to the cat, who circled him slowly for a careful look at its rescuer. "Between the two of us, I think you've fared better than I. For I've lost my place, lost my living, lost my supper, and had my nose punched into the bargain, all in the same day."

The white cat began sniffing Sebastian's fingers.

"Alas, I've nothing for you," Sebastian said. "Unless you're truly a witch, and conjure me up a roasted chicken and a new fiddle, I've nothing for myself either. I'll tell you truthfully, as things have gone with me, you'll do better to make your own way."

The cat, instead of taking Sebastian's advice, sat on its haunches and watched him boldly.

"Well, at least I'll do what I can for that ear of yours," Sebastian told him. "Come along, then."

Without warning, the cat suddenly tensed its muscles and leaped straight to Sebastian's shoulder, nearly knocking him off balance with the force of the spring.

"How now, are you cat or monkey?" Sebastian cried. "Let me know when you mean to play that trick again."

At the stream, he tore a bit of cloth from his shirt, dipped it in the water, and dabbed as gently as he could at the cat's injured ear. But after a moment, the cat struggled and twisted away to jump to the ground.

The animal moistened a forepaw with its tongue and painstakingly began scrubbing from the tips of its ears to the ends of its whiskers; then turned its attention to its muddy fur, licking it vigorously, ducking its head in every direction so as not to overlook any part of itself;

and all in all doing a more workmanlike job than Sebastian could have accomplished.

"Well, you're a handsome fellow, and make a better showing now than you did when first we met," Sebastian said, rubbing a finger under the cat's jaws. Bigger than it had seemed in the net, the cat's body was long, lean, sleek as an otter, and pure white from head to tail. Neck and shoulders were smoothly but powerfully muscled, the tips of the curving claws glittered like dagger points, and the cat's whole bearing was that of a wild creature more used to forests than to firesides.

Stroking the cat's head, Sebastian stopped when he touched the ridge of a heavy scar at the side of the animal's throat. "I can see you've been in more than one battle," he said, finding another long-healed wound under the fur of the cat's chest. "If you could talk, as those cowards in Dorn believed, you could surely tell me a few tales. Very well, if you mean to stay, make yourself comfortable. Though I doubt if I'll be able to do the same."

Sebastian gave his new friend a final pat and looked unhappily at the bushes that would have to serve as a bed.

Dusk was gathering quickly. Trampling the turf as smooth as he could, and longing for the Merry Host's bale of hay, Sebastian curled up awkwardly, with his green bag tucked under his head for a pillow.

He shut his eyes, hoping a night's sleep would be his best remedy. Instead, as he settled himself, the weight of the past day suddenly toppled on him. His nose throbbed, his head ached; and despite his brave words and bright hopes, with all his heart he wished himself back in the musicians' quarters, his hunger satisfied, his fiddle unbroken. Like a child, he tried to pretend that no disaster had really happened; that when he opened his eyes again, all would be as it had always been, with the First Fiddle shaking him out of bed; that The Purse, the Merry Host, Skimmerhorn, and Spargel were no more than a bad dream. Then he pressed his face into the makeshift pillow and wept as he had never done in all his life.

There was a faint rustling, and he started up. The cat had come to curl beside him, purring softly. Sebastian sank back and drew closer to the warmth of the furry body. In a while, he slept, holding the cat in his arms as if it were his last and only comfort; as indeed it was.

When he woke in the morning, his clothes were sopping with dew and he had a crick in his neck. But his spirits were higher than they had been the night before.

"Lost my living? No! My fiddle's ruined, that's true, and I can't buy another. But wherever I find a place, they'll have one I can borrow to prove my skill. And if I play well enough—why, they might make me a gift of any fiddle I want!"

Taking courage from this new thought, he jumped to his feet, waved his arms to shake off the morning chill and unknot his cramped muscles, and felt eager to start on his way again.

The cat had come bounding up from the stream. Sebastian clapped his hands and called out:

"Come along! With luck, I'll find a place for both of us. But hurry! *Hop-la! Presto! Prestissimo!*"

Without breaking stride, the cat leaped straight for Sebastian's shoulder, and clung there, purring happily, flirting its whiskers, and seeming to grin proudly at its own trick.

"Presto?" Sebastian repeated. "You're quick enough to be called that. Whatever your name before, if you had any at all, Presto you are and Presto you'll be."

With the cat draped like a white scarf over one shoulder and his green bag bouncing on the other, Sebastian set off in what he hoped was the direction of Spire. The crick in his neck had gone, but his appetite was roaring like a furnace; before he undertook to find a place, he would first have to find something to eat. The longer he walked, the hungrier he grew. His head pounded like a kettledrum and he felt a little giddy.

"I don't know how long it takes to starve," he said to the cat, "but I think I've well begun."

By this time of morning, he thought ruefully, Baron Purn-Hessel's cook would be handing him a second cup of chocolate and a third piece of cake; but these memories only sharpened his appetite. By the time he reached the outskirts of Spire, he was jogging along as fast as he could, ready to trade future fortune for present breakfast.

In his mind's ear, the name of Spire had rung like a golden bell in a golden steeple. Reaching the middle of the town, he found it not gold but gray. Though he had taken the precaution of carrying Presto in the green bag, for the cat's own safety as well as to avoid idle curiosity, he soon realized that he could have walked the narrow, muddy streets with Presto perched on top of his head, for all the folk of Spire would have noticed. Housewives with market baskets, soldiers with pistols in their belts and sabers rattling at their sides, tradesmen, and shabbily dressed children jostled along with never a glance at him. The faces of the passersby seemed pinched and tightly drawn. They kept their eyes straight ahead, looking neither left nor right, and hurried anxiously on their way.

To Sebastian's disappointment, the opera house and theatre had been closed and turned into barracks for a new garrison of the Regent's dragoons. He learned this from the first passerby he ventured to ask: a carpenter who seemed frightened out of his wits at being stopped and questioned, who stammered out the information most unwillingly and set off again with all speed.

Sebastian shook his head. The air of Spire had begun to weigh on him and make him as uneasy as the rest of the townsfolk. "Did I ever hope to find a place here?" he muttered to Presto, who peered up at him from the depths of the bag. "Why, it seems worth a man's neck to give you the time of day! And that poor devil of a carpenter—you might have thought I was the Regent himself, he was so glad to be shut of me! Well, no matter. Darmstel's bound to have better cheer. In any case, it surely can't be worse."

Before pressing on, however, Sebastian realized he would have to answer his appetite or collapse on the spot. His eyes brightened at the sight of a bakeshop and he stepped inside, joining the crowd of errand boys, housewives, and servant girls elbowing each other for places at the counter.

The flour-daubed baker and his apprentice shoveled hot loaves from the oven; the baker-woman, as stout as if she had risen with her own yeast, was selling her wares so quickly that Sebastian feared none would be left when it came his turn. He waited impatiently, drinking in the aroma, delighting himself by trying to decide between a long, a round, or a square loaf, tasting each in his imagination.

Finally at the counter, he was too hungry to care about shape and simply pointed eagerly at the biggest loaf he saw, crisp and golden-crusted, looking half the size of a millstone. His face fell, however, when he reached into his pocket. His fingers found only a ragged hole, torn, most likely, during the scuffle at the Merry Host. His coins were gone.

"My money—I can't find it," he stammered as the baker-woman held out her hand. Hastily, he pulled all his pockets inside out, hoping the coins were only misplaced. The search yielded nothing.

The baker-woman snatched back the loaf as if it were the crown jewels of Hamelin-Loring. "Go play your jokes elsewhere," she cried, "and let honest folk be served."

The crowd behind him grumbled, jostled, and called for him to step aside. Sebastian, roughly shoved from the counter, turned to the baker.

"My money's lost, but I'll pay with my work," he offered. "Let me clean your oven, or sweep—"

The baker looked at him suspiciously. "What's your trade?"

"I'm a fiddler," Sebastian began. "But—"

"Then go fiddle!" returned the baker. "I say: a place for every man and every man in his place. And why you're out of yours is no business of mine."

So saying, the baker went back to plying his long-handled wooden shovel, pulling loaf after loaf out of the oven.

Baffled, Sebastian lingered at the fringe of the crowd.

The smell of bread made his head spin and his mouth water. He breathed deeply, trying to feed on the delicious odor, but this made him only hungrier. Near the counter, a trestle table held a large mixing bowl, a basin of flour, and a pot of butter. Amid these he glimpsed a basket of eggs that drew him like a lodestone. He edged his way to the table.

For long moments he gazed wistfully at the smooth, shining eggs, which now appeared the most beautiful objects he had ever seen. He tasted them soft-boiled, hard-boiled, fried, poached, beaten into an omelette, or even raw. He set his teeth, trying to pull himself away. While serving Baron Purn-Hessel, he would never have hesitated a moment to make free of any dainties lying on the Chief Cook's table; in fact, he often suspected the cook left them there on purpose to be snatched away. But Spire, as he was all too well aware, was not the Baron's estate. The eggs were the baker's, not the Chief Cook's.

Sebastian's fingers twitched, his hands trembled in fear. Try as he would, he could not turn his eyes from the eggs, which grew bigger, brighter, and tastier the longer he stared at them. At last, his hunger overcame his conscience. He could struggle no more. Glancing over his shoulder, he stepped closer to the table, seized three of the eggs, and slipped them into his shirt.

He could not resist a fourth. As he picked it up, the baker's boy spied him and cried:

"Stop, thief!"

v ⚬ How a Friend Found Sebastian

Ꮪᴇʙᴀꜱᴛɪᴀɴ froze in guilty terror. The baker, shovel still in hand, spun around as the apprentice cried out again and pointed accusingly.

In panic, Sebastian dashed for the bakeshop door and burst into the street, with the baker, the baker's wife, and the apprentice behind him.

The errand boys, housewives, and servant girls streamed after, shouting "Stop, thief!" at the tops of their voices, although none had any clear notion what had been stolen.

Sebastian raced ahead, skidded around a corner, pumping his legs for all they were worth, while passersby joined the chase, adding their voices to the clamor. Catching sight of an alleyway, he darted for it in a last hope of escaping the furious baker. Just as he reached it and was about to plunge into the shadows, from the mouth of the alley came a workman trundling a wheelbarrow.

Too late to veer aside, Sebastian made a desperate leap; but not high enough. His legs tangled with the handles, the barrow toppled over, and with it Sebastian, who pitched headlong. The eggs inside his shirt splattered against the cobbles.

The baker was on him in a trice, flailing the long-handled shovel, belaboring him about the head and shoulders while the onlookers pressed closer, bawling and bellowing as loudly as they could:

"Fetch the sergeant of guards!"

"Call out the dragoons!"

"Beware! He's got a pistol!"

The baker flailed all the harder. Sebastian covered his head with his arms and flung himself on the green bag, trying to shield Presto from the hail of blows.

"Stop!" a voice commanded.

The baker halted, shovel in midair. Sebastian ventured to raise his head. Instead of a watchman or guard, as he expected, he saw a stout little man making his way through the crowd. His ruddy cheeks were as plump as those of the cherubs painted on Baron Purn-Hessel's ceiling; his sparse brown hair hung down about his ears, and he blinked around him with a pair of blue eyes as innocent and guileless as a baby's.

"Now then," he said, setting down a lumpy knapsack, "whatever can be amiss?"

"Caught a thief," the baker proudly replied. "Broke into my shop in broad daylight, the bold rogue."

"Indeed? " said the stranger, curiously. "And what, sir, might he have stolen?"

"What's he stolen?" the baker cried indignantly. "Why, the best part of a dozen eggs!"

The stranger pursed his lips and rolled up his eyes at this shocking and horrifying news. "An egg-stealer! A grave and weighty matter." He turned to Sebastian. "Is this true?"

Sebastian, whose face burned with shame and humiliation, silently nodded.

The stranger continued. "And what did you mean to do with them?"

Sebastian hung his head. "Eat them," he murmured.

The stranger clicked his tongue and looked still more shocked. "Since these eggs are broken, you obviously can't give them back. Since you stole them in the first place, I doubt if you can pay for them." He reached into his pocket and turned to the baker. "Perhaps the matter can be gently settled. Now, sir, if you'd kindly tell me what your eggs cost?"

"A ducat," the baker hastily declared. "Every bit of a ducat."

"So high?" returned the man, astonished. "In Loringhold itself, eggs go begging at half that price; in New Locking and Upper Hamelin, even less. And here in Spire—ask any housewife what she'd pay." He frowned in deep concern. "Why, friend, can it be that whoever sold you those eggs charged you too dear? And played you for a fool?"

The baker's face reddened as it dawned on him he had been caught in his own trap. No matter what he replied, he would have to admit himself either a fool or a liar. The onlookers, at first altogether on the side of the baker, now nudged one another and chuckled at his discomfort.

The baker's wife pushed forward and whispered in her husband's ear:

"Hold your tongue! You're a blockhead and always were! You've lost the eggs, now you'll lose the price of them."

Changing her angry frown to a wheedling smile, she turned to the stranger. "If the kind gentleman means to take it on himself to pay us, with a little added for our pains—"

The man drew out a handful of coppers, smiled blandly, bowed as gracefully as any courtier, and presented the coins to the baker's wife, who giggled and simpered at the unexpected gallantry.

The bystanders, seeing their sport ended, went about their business. The baker's wife, berating her husband under her breath, seized the apprentice by the ear and turned back toward the shop.

Sebastian climbed to his feet. Yolks and whites poured from his sopping shirt. Presto, at least, was unharmed in the bag. Still shamefaced, Sebastian bowed to his rescuer and murmured his thanks.

The stranger grinned broadly. "That baker has a heavy hand, and I'd hate to be the dough in his kneading trough. But now, sir, would you care to tell me whose skin I was able to save—what's left of it, anyway. In short, who are you?"

"Who am I?" Sebastian replied bitterly. "I'm a thief, as you've seen for yourself. A brawler, a troublemaker, a rebel, and a renegade—so I've been called, so that's very likely what I am."

The man raised his eyebrows. "All that at once? Then I assume you're on your way to be hanged? Meantime, if you're as hungry as you say, you'll need more than a shirtful of empty eggshells. Come along, then, and see if your appetite's bigger than your villainy."

Sebastian gratefully nodded. "So I will, and my thanks to you. But—who are you?"

"I? Why, I suppose you might call me Nicholas."

VI ❧ How Sebastian Heard of the Captain

ELL, then, Master Nicholas," returned Sebastian, "I owe you the cost of a clutch of eggs, and promise to repay —indeed, if I manage to earn that much. Though I'll tell you truthfully, the way things stand with me now, I'm beginning to wonder if I ever will."

Rubbing his neck and shoulders, and smarting as much from shame as from the bread-shovel, Sebastian followed his benefactor along the streets of Spire, explaining how he had come to lose his place and what had happened to him since leaving Baron Purn-Hessel's service.

"I only wish I were back again," he said glumly. "I've met a sour-hearted innkeeper who called himself Merry, a pair of bullies who told me a white cat was black, a baker who'd do well as a highwayman; and yours is the only friendly face I've seen so far in Hamelin-Loring. The thing that puzzles me is why you took my part."

Nicholas grinned at him. "I'd not stand by and see a feather mattress beaten so soundly. And surely not see a lad carted off to meet the hangman."

"Hangman?" Sebastian repeated. "What, do you mean to tell me an egg's worth a dance on the gallows?"

Nicholas nodded unhappily. "So it is, alas. Since the Regent's come to power, we'd all best tread carefully around his new laws, for there's hardly one that doesn't have a noose at the end of it."

Sebastian's jaw dropped. Realizing how narrow his escape had been, he began shaking and trembling with both fright and indignation, even more dismayed after the fact then he had been before it.

"Ah, Nicholas," he murmured, "I see my debt's bigger than I thought. Saved my skin? Why, friend, you've saved my neck!"

Nicholas only looked embarrassed by Sebastian's gratitude. By this time they had reached the end of a flight of cobbled steps, and here, under a stone bridge, Nicholas unstrapped his pack.

"Now then," he said, "we'll see what's here for you— the two of you," he added, blinking at Presto, who had worked the drawstrings loose with his claws and now popped his head out of the green bag.

While Presto rubbed against the little man's legs as happily as if they had been old friends met again, Sebastian hurried to the riverside, peeled off his egg-soaked shirt, and rinsed it out as best he could. Changing into a fresh garment, he went back to the bridge, where Nicholas had built a small fire of charcoal and spitted a good share of meat over it. He was astonished to see Nicholas also produce from his pack a bottle of wine, a couple of tin cups, and a loaf of bread which he cut into thick slices with a curious pocket knife of a dozen different blades. Though Presto chewed daintily at a slice of the meat, Sebastian was too famished to follow his cat's example, and wolfed down his own portion, finding it more delicious than any dish ever to come from Baron Purn-Hessel's kitchen.

"So it turns out you're not a villian but a fiddler," Nicholas remarked, after finishing his meal and setting a stumpy clay pipe between his teeth. "If your heart's set on music, you'll no doubt find a place one way or another."

Sebastian shrugged. "It's not that my heart's set on fiddling, it's all my fingers know how to do. Lucky that I have some skill at my trade, but I'd not mind changing it if I found another I could do as well. As for your own trade, I had meant to ask you, but there's no need. For I can guess you're a cook, and the best I've met!"

Nicholas smiled and shook his head. "My concern's not with cookery but with reaching Darmstel before nightfall. As it happens, I have some acquaintance with the innkeeper of the Golden Stag there. If you care to travel along with me, he might let you sleep a night under his roof."

Sebastian gladly accepted this offer, hoping his misfortunes at last were ended. Nicholas quickly and deftly stowed away all his gear and slung his pack once more on his back. With his hunger satisfied, his spirits beginning to rise again, and with Presto stretched over his shoulder, Sebastian followed him along the riverbank. Nicholas stepped out briskly and jauntily, surprisingly so for one of his girth, and Sebastian was hard pressed to keep pace with his new friend.

To quicken his gait, Sebastian set to whistling a tune; and was amazed once again to see his comrade reach into his jacket and pull out a pair of well-worn, yellowed ivory tubes, which he fitted together to make a flute. Nicholas put the instrument to his lips, quickly caught the tune Sebastian was whistling, and not only followed it but added dancing, skipping variations of his own.

"Bravo!" cried Sebastian. "You may be a shrewd judge of the price of eggs, and a cook who turns plain meat into a banquet, but now I see you're truly a piper! With better skill than Baron Purn-Hessel's First Flute!"

"A piper? Not I," Nicholas answered modestly. "Oh, I've played here and there to meet a moment's need; but more for my liking than my living. I'd rather pipe my own measures and set my own time and tune."

Saying no more, Nicholas led them from the riverside path across open fields to the Royal Highway. This was so badly rutted and pocked all over with holes that Sebastian declared:

"Royal road? Then I'd hate to follow the common one! I wonder if even the Regent dares make his way over it!"

"I should say he's happier to line his pockets with tolls and taxes," replied Nicholas. "Under his new decrees, every highway and byway belongs to him. Now, when a drover takes his cattle to market, he must pay dearly for each mile of road he travels. And so must every carter and coachman—and since there's no roads but the Regent's, they've hardly a choice in the matter. And by the time they've paid the fees, they've little profit from their work."

"There's no justice in that," Sebastian declared. "Nor even good sense. But those matters are beyond me. Alas, there's nothing a common fiddler can do about it. Indeed, the last time I spoke up to the nobility I lost my place."

Since his words only reminded him of past misfortune, Sebastian turned his thoughts to more hopeful prospects in Darmstel. The day was bright and clear; and having feasted his stomach, he now feasted his ears on the bird-songs in the wooded fields, the cowbells of distant herds, and the rhythm of his own strides over the loose-packed road.

Presto, as they went along, would often hop down from Sebastian's shoulder and go bounding into the tall weeds beside the highway, pouncing at shadows or scuttling up a tree, as the mood struck him. But the cat never let his master out of his sight. Before the travelers could go too far, Presto would leave off his games and race to catch up with Sebastian. When they stopped to rest, Presto sometimes turned kittenish and rolled on his back in the dust; at others, purring loudly, he rubbed back and forth against Sebastian's shins. When Presto curled on his lap, Sebastian would lovingly stroke the cat's ears, ruffle the fur under the powerful jaws, and all the while call him whatever fondly nonsensical name struck his fancy: His Most Excellent Catliness, The Black Witch of Dorn, Prince of Meows, or His Excellency the Duke of Gauli-Mauli.

Thus they lightened each other's journey and the day passed quickly. A little way from Darmstel, the travelers met half-a-dozen road menders toiling with picks and mattocks, and Sebastian called out: "Do your work well, friends! The Regent's road is no easy one for walking."

"Ride, then," called back one of the road menders, a broad-faced, hard-muscled man, shirtless like his comrades.

"Better yet, stay at home," put in another. He turned

to his companion. "That's where I'd rather be, Andreas. My field will be a mudhole by the time I get back to it."

"What about my vines?" returned the man called Andreas. "I'll be lucky to have a handful of sour raisins at harvest."

Sebastian grinned at them. "From your talk, friends, you know more about fields and vines than you do of your trade."

"Our trade?" cried Andreas, angrily flinging down his mattock. "We're farmers and grape growers, all. We mend roads for a month each spring and fall. The Regent's law binds us to do it willy-nilly but doesn't put a penny in our pockets for labor lost. Most of my harvest barely pays the land tax, and the salt tax, and the seed tax. Grinssorg will soon have our bones as well as the skin off them. Curse him, I say—"

"Hold your tongue, Andreas," muttered the farmer. "You don't know who you're dealing with. The Regent's bloodhounds have long noses and sharp ears."

"Bloodhounds?" retorted Andreas. "The one looks hardly dry behind his own ears; and the other, a harmless fellow."

"Maybe so, maybe not," said the farmer. "Don't forget the two poor devils in Darmstel, hanged for speaking out against the Regent."

"Rather a rope around my neck than a gag in my mouth," declared Andreas. "I'll speak my mind, no matter if the Regent himself hears me."

After what he had seen of the frightened folk in Spire, the boldness of the grape grower surprised Sebastian, and he looked at the open-faced Andreas with lively admiration.

"Take me for no bloodhound," he declared. "If it hadn't been for my friend, I'd be swinging on the Regent's gallows by now."

Nicholas, meanwhile, had sat down on a boulder, with his short legs stretched out before him, and was mopping his face with a yellow handkerchief pulled from his sleeve. But, hearing the grape grower's words, he blinked his eyes in concern, and said:

"Two hanged in Darmstel? Now that seems to me a great pity, for the little you say they did."

"A pity?" Andreas burst out. "A crime! It's murder out and out! The Regent grinds us till we creak, then kills us into the bargain. Alas, even Captain Freeling couldn't save them."

"Captain Freeling?" put in Sebastian. "Who's that?"

"Have you been living on the moon?" replied Andreas. "Not heard of the Captain? Why, I think he's the only one to help us against Grinssorg. No one knows his real name, but he's the very devil of a fellow, tall as a tree, with a great black mustache—"

"That's not true," interrupted the farmer. "The Captain's not dark, but yellow-headed. My cousin's brother-in-law saw him face to face, and he'll not forget the sight. The fellow's eyes flash like blue lightning—"

Andreas snorted. "Much your cousin's brother-in-law knows. The Captain's swarthy, his hair black as pitch. He can break a man in two with his bare hands. The Regent's put a price of a thousand ducats on his head, and half that on each of his followers."

Nicholas, listening attentively, shook his head in wonder. "Whatever color his hair, he must be a bold rogue indeed. Do you mean to tell me, sir, that he's to be found in Darmstel?"

"In Darmstel?" replied Andreas. "In Spire, Great Brunswick, and some say in Loringhold itself. Here, there, everywhere! Not one of Grinssorg's bloodhounds or dragoons can lay him by the heels, for he's gone as fast as he's come. Break open the tax coffers one day and scatter ducats to the poor; snatch a man from the gallows the next, quick as the wind, north at dawn, south at night. You're a green traveler if you've not heard of him."

"Heard of him? That I have, sir," answered Nicholas, "but not so far into the country. They say he has a band of a dozen stout fellows like him."

"Ten score, most likely," corrected Andreas. "And more power to him! Should he ever need another to join him, Andreas is his man. So are half the able bodies in Darmstel. Let him give the signal to rise against Grinssorg, and we'll hear it plain enough."

"And so will I!" Sebastian cried. "Indeed, I'll not wait for his signal, but seek him out myself!"

VII ❧ How Sebastian Had a Bucket on His Head

THE idea so fired Sebastian's imagination that he saw himself already mounted on a high-spirited stallion galloping across the countryside. Ready to set off instantly, he clapped Nicholas on the back and cried:

"Did I say a fiddler could do nothing against the Regent? Here's my chance! I'd sooner ride with the Captain than scrape away in some noble idiot's orchestra! And you, my friend, come along! We'll find the Captain and both join him!"

But Nicholas, instead of eagerly agreeing, only looked uncomfortable. "The Captain—ah, well, now, there's no doubt he's a bold fellow to challenge the Regent. As for joining him, that's a different matter. It's not a quiet life, with a price on your head and the Regent's dragoons on your heels."

While saying this, he took Sebastian's arm and began gently but firmly leading him along the highway again, at a faster pace than before. Sebastian fell silent, disappointed at his friend's reluctance. Much as he would hate to part from Nicholas, he nevertheless resolved to seek out the Captain one way or another.

The road menders were soon far behind. But if Nicholas had seemed anxious to reach Darmstel quickly, the closer he came to the town the more unwilling he appeared to enter it.

"You're a strange traveler," Sebastian remarked, puzzled, as Nicholas deliberately turned off the road at the very outskirts of Darmstel and began making his way along hedges and across ditches. "I grant you the Royal Highway's not very royal and not very much of a way, but I like it better than crawling through brambles."

By now, they were approaching the town from an altogether different direction. No sooner did Sebastian glimpse the market square than Nicholas halted and drew back once again. Half-a-dozen dragoons stood by their horses at the watering trough, while a couple more loitered by the shop fronts. Looking closer, Sebastian realized there were still others at the street corners.

"Nicholas, what's amiss?" he murmured uneasily.

"Two hangings, as the road mender told us," Nicholas answered grimly. "But that's far from the end of it. Two lives? Not enough to satisfy Grinssorg. His bloodhounds are surely trying to ferret out the poor devils' friends and families. And anyone else who might side against the Regent."

"And the townsfolk? They'll do nothing?"

"They may try, but the dragoons are there to put down whatever trouble starts. And they'll stop and search every stranger they see in Darmstel. Since I don't relish standing against a wall with a dragoon's bayonet in my ribs and my pockets turned inside out—we'd better wait for a while."

"A shame the Captain isn't here," Sebastian exclaimed.

"He'd be more than a match for a whole company of dragoons."

Nicholas shrugged and said no more, and not until dusk was he willing to venture into the town. Though the streets, by now, had fallen into heavy shadow and lights glimmered only here and there, he found his way to the Golden Stag with surprising ease. And so quickly that Sebastian wondered if his strange friend could see as well as Presto in the dark.

Unlike the Merry Host, the proprietor of the Golden Stag appeared open-faced and good-natured; and, as Nicholas had foretold, he was willing to give Sebastian not only lodging for the night but supper, too. While Presto crouched by the fireplace and surveyed the company with as much satisfaction as if he were the host, Sebastian sat down to his meal. Nicholas, meanwhile, had begun some private conversation with the innkeeper. Sebastian could neither overhear nor guess the subject of their talk, but Nicholas frowned in concern and the innkeeper appeared tense and uneasy. Although the eating room was filled, the guests showed no sign of good cheer, but spoke either in low voices or not at all, and their expressions were half-bitter, half-brooding.

This mood of the Golden Stag, instead of raising Sebastian's spirits, only turned his thoughts inward; and he admitted to himself that he truly had no clear idea what to do next. Absorbed in trying to sort out all that had happened to him in so short a time, and to set some plan for the future, he was startled by a voice in his ear:

"Traveled some distance, your honor?"

It was Sebastian's table mate who had spoken: a foppishly dressed man, somewhat less than middle height, with a close-shaven, puffy face pale as a fish belly, and with a jaunty spray of lace for a neckcloth. The stranger wore no wig, but his drab hair was so fancily twirled and teased that Sebastian could hardly tell the difference; and about the fellow hung a cloying scent of pomades, lotions, and aromatic ointments.

"Why, so I have," Sebastian replied, "and I suppose I have still farther to go."

"At your service, then, your worship," said the man, smiling and bending most humbly and fawningly. "Would you be shaved? Your hair powdered? A tooth drawn? Blood let?" His fingers, very fleshy and flexible, meantime were deftly undoing the buckles of a black leather case, which opened to reveal not only bottles of perfume and cakes of soap, but also an assortment of lancets, razors, a jar of squirming leeches, and a number of glittering, cruel-looking surgical instruments.

"Spare your pains and mine," Sebastian answered, grimacing at the leeches. "I need none of those bloodsuckers or tooth pullers. My thanks to you, all the same."

"Another time, then, your worship," said the dapper barber-surgeon, taking Sebastian's arm. "But tell me now, your honor, how did you fare along the roads? Have you just come to Darmstel? An easy journey? On foot, did you say?"

"On my two feet, indeed," Sebastian ruefully replied. "If you could see them, you'd not have to guess. I think I gained three blisters for every half-league."

"Ah?" said the barber, clicking his tongue sympathetically. "You suffer from vesicular bullification. A common complaint."

"I should think so, for anyone who walks the Royal

Highway," Sebastian said. "I'd call it a golden road for none but the Regent."

The barber pursed his lips and raised his eyebrows. "Now it's curious your worship comes to that conclusion. Do you say the Regent profits at the expense of his own subjects?"

"So I say, and so does everyone," Sebastian replied. "The Regent has both hands in everybody's pockets. Or around their throats."

The barber sighed. "Yes, your worship, I suppose the times do pinch in Hamelin-Loring."

"Choke, you might say," retorted Sebastian. "Pinch is putting it too gently."

"Well, your worship, you seem a gentleman of spirit —and a gay blade with the ladies, too, your honor, I'll be bound—so you should have no trouble making your way. But where is your way, did you mention?"

"That I don't know," Sebastian answered, "though I wish I did." In spite of his obsequious manner, the barber appeared eager to be friendly; and Sebastian was by no means displeased at being called "your worship" and "your honor" and being taken for a dashing gentleman, after all the insults from the Merry Host and the baker. And so he continued, as a thought suddenly came to him, lowering his voice and saying to the barber:

"When I was on the road, I heard some talk of a Captain Freeling. He needs good men to follow him, but no one's sure where to find him. Now, surely you're better-traveled than I am, and you might know something of this Captain?"

The barber frowned and shook his head. "Why, your honor, you could likely tell me more than I could tell you. Exactly and precisely what has your worship heard? There's loose tongues in Hamelin-Loring, all ready to wag with no truth whatever. Who was it, in fact, spoke of the Captain? And where? These little details, your honor, might help you sift fact from idle gossip."

Before Sebastian could answer, the innkeeper came up quickly to say that the house was crowded and if he hoped for a bed he would be well advised to find one without delay.

Taking leave of the barber, Sebastian hurried up the stairs, with Presto bounding after. The chamber to which the innkeeper had directed him was already over-flowing with travelers. Sebastian went on to the next, opened the door, and peered in. The room was small and stuffy, with half a candle burning in a saucer on the table. A bucket of wash water stood in a corner. As far as Sebastian could see, however, there was only one occupant, stretched out on a straw pallet: a fellow who had gone to bed without having gone to the trouble of undressing.

Pleased by his good luck at finding a single bedmate in-stead of half a dozen, he stepped inside and called out good-naturedly, "Now, friend, I don't like to disturb your sleeping, since you're doing so well at it; but there's room for another if you'd be so good as to shove yourself over a little."

His bedfellow made no reply beyond burying his head deeper into the bolster.

Sebastian repeated his request. As there was still no an-swer, he urged:

"Come now, let's have a place there, too. No need to be selfish in the matter of a little straw."

So saying, he sat down on the narrow edge of the pallet

and without further ado began to unbutton his jacket, deciding that one way or another he would have a share of the bed, for he was bone-weary after the day's long tramp.

The fellow stirred, and slipped away to the side.

"That's better, and I thank you," Sebastian called over his shoulder, still in the midst of pulling off his jacket. "Share and share alike makes good companions."

An instant later, Sebastian was sitting on the floor, gasping and choking under a flood of cold water, with the bucket on his head.

VIII ❧ How Sebastian Misjudged His Opponent

SPUTTERING and shouting indignantly, Sebastian flung off the bucket and scrambled to his feet. His jacket, shirt, and breeches were sopping, and water had poured even into his boots. His fellow traveler had meanwhile backed against the wall.

"Is that your notion of a joke?" Sebastian cried. "It's not mine! Come out of that corner and fight like a man!"

In answer, his chamber mate reached out and fetched him a sharp box on the ear.

All the more furious at being so smartly buffeted, in addition to being kept from his bed and soaked to the skin, Sebastian put up his fists. His adversary, with much reluctance, raised his hands defensively but made no move to leave the protection of the corner.

"So, so!" cried Sebastian. "You've played your prank. Now you'll pay for it!"

Just then, the door burst open and Nicholas hurried into the room. Behind him crowded the innkeeper and a handful of guests, some already in their nightcaps, others drawn from the eating room by Sebastian's indignant outcries.

"Gently, gently," commanded Nicholas. "Have done, both of you. There's no quarrel that can't be quietly settled."

By repeated assurances there had been no bloodshed, nor likelihood of any, Nicholas soon succeeded in dispersing the onlookers, among them the barber, who had come with his case under his arm, sniffing out possible business and hopeful that his ministrations would be needed.

Sebastian, during this, had calmed down enough to look closer at his adversary. Instead of a grown man, he saw a lad fully a head shorter than himself, whose long and disheveled black hair tumbled over a pale, frightened face. The boy's jacket was of excellent quality but outrageous fit, for it reached below his knees, nearly as long as his breeches, which had been belted up as far as they would go. The shirt was a fine white lawn, but meant for a stouter wearer, and the youth seemed ready at any moment to disappear into his clothes.

"Well, and what have we here?" exclaimed Sebastian. "A pup? A cub? Now, my lad, you've had a narrow escape. You might have been pounded to a pulp! Let that be a lesson for you, trifling with your elders."

Nicholas stepped closer to the boy, and said in a quiet voice, "No harm will come to you, and surely not from my excitable friend here. But you've run risk enough in traveling alone."

"Yes, and you'd better do as I tell you," put in Sebastian. "I can see at a glance you're a runaway apprentice of one sort or another. So, hurry back to your master."

At this, Nicholas began to chuckle. "An apprentice? I

should hardly think so. A runaway? Yes, I should say for certain that she is."

"She?" Sebastian repeated. "She? Nicholas, you've gone out of your wits, taking a baker's boy or printer's devil for a girl."

Nicholas grinned at him. "Had you looked a little closer, you'd have known it from the first. Her jacket's belted wrong side to, for one thing. And is there a boy older than a baby who'd make a fist with his thumb tucked under his fingers?"

Sebastian gaped in astonishment, realizing Nicholas had spoken the truth. The uncropped hair was indeed too long for a boy's, and the features too smooth and finely drawn.

"Ah—ah, well, of course," Sebastian stammered, reluctant to admit he had been doubly fooled. "I'd have seen it for myself in another moment. It strikes the eye! A runaway goosegirl or kitchenmaid. To think she almost traded blows with me, skinny and scrawny as she is!"

The girl gasped with indignation.

Nicholas clucked his tongue placatingly, and said, "Oh, I doubt if those white hands ever fed geese or scraped pots."

He pursed his lips and shook his head, as though dismayed by his own observation.

"No matter what she is," replied Sebastian, "the Golden Stag's no place for her." He turned to the girl. "Now, missy, tell us what brought you here and you'll have our help in setting matters right."

The girl raised her head and, looking straight at Sebastian, declared in a very earnest and dignified tone:

"Sir, in future and presumably more favorable circumstances, your courtesy shall be both gratefully remembered and appropriately recompensed. Be assured also that the emptying of that receptacle was the result of momentary confusion, and should not be construed as indicating ill intent or deliberate malice. However, since you offer to be of service, your most accommodating and expedient course will be, sir, to depart from these premises."

"What?" Sebastian burst out. "We mean to help you—but if I understand half what you're saying, you're telling us to be off!"

The girl looked calmly at him with cool, deep green eyes.

"If the suggestion is unacceptable," she declared, "the only remaining alternative must be assumed."

So saying, she turned and strode to the door.

Nicholas, with astonishing spryness, hustled ahead of her. Though his brow wrinkled apologetically, and his mild eyes blinked so that he looked like a flustered and embarrassed cherub, he planted himself solidly at the doorway and showed no intention of moving from that spot.

"Now, now, now," he murmured hastily. "A delicate matter, that's true, and likely none of my business at all. But it scrapes my conscience to see any lass alone and undefended. And more so, when the lass happens to be Princess Isabel of Hamelin-Loring."

IX ∽ How the Travelers Began a Hasty Departure

NICHOLAS bowed courteously to the girl, who stopped in her tracks and glanced around, much distressed, for another way out of the chamber.

Sebastian stared at her, and clapped his hands to his head. "An apprentice boy turns into a princess? Ah, no, Nicholas, she can't be!"

"She is," Nicholas replied. "I knew her in spite of those breeches. She's been lucky so far, if no one else has recognized her. But it puzzles me to see her in a garret instead of the Glorietta."

Finding no escape, the Princess drew herself up stiffly and declared:

"Inasmuch as our intention is to maintain ourselves in strictest incognito, the recognition of our identity represents a most unfortunate occurrence. Nevertheless, an essential question remains to be considered: Whether your original proposal of assistance to the individual you had erroneously esteemed to be a custodian of domestic fowl continues to be extended to us in our quality of Princess of Hamelin-Loring. If it does, you may serve us best either by your silence regarding our present situation; or by divulging further means of hastening our journey to Upper Cassel, the realm of our uncle, Prince Frederick William."

Sebastian had still not overcome his bewilderment, and this new pronouncement threw him into deeper confusion. "Journey?" he exclaimed. "To Upper Cassel? But . . . but I've heard with my own ears that you're to wed the Regent."

Nicholas gave Isabel a curious glance. "I've heard the same, Your Grace. And so it seems to me that Your Grace should be more concerned with choosing a bridal gown than wearing a pair of breeches."

"It is not our intention to marry," the Princess burst out. "And if it were, assuredly we would never consent to such a union. Count Grinssorg became Regent after our parents' death. Since then, he has done all in his power to break our realm to his will. Now that we have reached an age to ascend the throne ourselves and put an end to his regency, he dared to ask our hand in marriage.

"Naturally, we refused. Count Grinssorg is avaricious, rapacious, heartless, and as Prince of Hamelin-Loring would be the greatest disaster to our realm. But when he learned we would not accept marriage with him, he flew into a rage and vowed he would have either our hand or our life.

"We determined, therefore, to flee the Glorietta. Our first duty being the welfare of our devoted subjects, we see no course except that of reaching Upper Cassel and requesting Prince Frederick to place his army at our command for the purpose of overthrowing the Regent. It would also be our duty to lead these gallant combatants to a victory both decisive and well-deserved."

Through this long account, the Princess seemed at a loss for neither words nor breath. And after hearing her declaration to march at the head of an army, Sebastian could not make up his mind whether Isabel was the bravest girl he had ever met or completely out of her wits.

Nicholas, who had been listening intently, shook his head with serious concern. "Now, Your Grace," he said, "if all this is true as you tell it, I doubt you'll get even half the way to Upper Cassel. If the Regent means to seize the throne, he'll have you back alive or dead; and, I daresay, by choice the latter. You can be certain every one of his spies and bloodhounds in Hamelin-Loring seeks you this very moment."

"We are sensible of that fact, sir," Isabel replied. "But you must also apprehend that the Regent will proceed with utmost circumspection. It would not be to his advantage to let our flight from the Glorietta become widely known. Whatever their nefarious actions against our person, his agents must perform them secretly. Even the Regent would prefer to assume no responsibility for our disappearance or demise."

The little man nodded agreement. "It would suit the Regent if you vanished altogether; or met, shall we say, with an unfortunate accident. But you, Princess, run a terrible risk if you trust the help of strangers." He blinked at her. "Why, can you even be sure whether I myself wish you well or ill?"

"Of course you wish her well!" Sebastian exclaimed. "And we'll help all we can. I've no love for the Regent and neither have you. I know nothing of armies, courts, thrones, or what have you. But one way or another, she must get safely out of Hamelin-Loring."

Before he could speak further, the Princess caught sight of Presto, calmly observing all the goings-on.

"That is a cat," she said, in the first simple and straightforward comment Sebastian had heard from her since their encounter. "The Regent's Court Councillor of Natural Philosophy favored us with a number of statements regarding these creatures. The cat, unlike members of the canine race, is by nature willful and intractable. The Court Councillor of Natural Philosophy drew the conclusion therefrom that the cat was a most unsuitable animal to be associated with a reigning monarch."

Sebastian clapped a hand to his head, scarcely believing that the Princess, in mortal danger, would give any thought whatever to a court councillor's speculations about cats and dogs.

"We have not been permitted the company of felines," Isabel continued, in a wistful voice, "although it would have been our pleasure to observe their nature and behavior."

"A Princess, and not allowed to keep a cat?" Sebastian began.

"Once we had a stray kitten," Isabel replied, "that made its way somehow into our chamber. But the Regent found it with us and strangled it before our eyes, to demonstrate how a monarch should display power over his subjects."

"Why, not even the cats of Hamelin-Loring are safe from Grinssorg!" Sebastian cried.

"Come now," Nicholas interrupted, shouldering his pack. "If Your Grace wants help, I'll give mine as willingly as my friend. I'll have a word with the innkeeper, for I think none of us should stay here longer than need be."

Taking Presto under one arm and his bag under the other, Sebastian followed Nicholas and Princess Isabel down the stairs. The eating room was empty, save for the barber, snoring away in a corner, as though hopeful to the last of finding someone requiring hairdressing, tooth-drawing, or bloodletting.

Seeing nothing of the innkeeper, Nicholas gestured for the Princess and Sebastian to go outside, where he led them briskly but quietly across the dark innyard to the stables. Presto, wriggling from his master's hold, padded ahead.

In the stables, Nicholas dropped his pack and began hauling at the shafts of a small wagon. Sebastian was about to help him when he heard Presto yowl and hiss in alarm. The cat had darted into one of the empty stalls. Sebastian hurried after him.

In the moonlight, he saw Presto with his tail bushed out and ears close against his head. Sebastian's foot caught on something in the straw and nearly tripped him up. He bent, then cried out in horror.

Lying flat on his back, his mouth gaping, the inn-keeper stared up at him. The man's face was bloodless except for a crimson daub like a gay neckerchief where his throat had been slashed.

x ☙ How Nicholas Became a Royal Tailor

$\mathcal{S}$EBASTIAN's cry brought Nicholas running, with Isabel close after.

"Take the girl away from this," Nicholas commanded as he knelt by the innkeeper and sought vainly for a sign of life.

The Princess clapped a hand to her mouth; her cheeks paled and her eyes wavered. Sebastian felt his own knees tremble and his head start echoing and spinning as if he himself were about to turn up his toes. Nevertheless, he managed to catch hold of her before she toppled. He found the Princess to be astonishingly light in his arms, yet he could barely stagger to the innyard, where he lowered Isabel to the cobbles, and wondered desperately what he should do about a Princess unconscious at his feet and a murdered man in the stable.

That moment, he glimpsed the barber coming from the doorway of the Golden Stag.

"Help, ho!" Sebastian cried, glad to see the foppish fellow even with his nauseating leeches and lancets.

"Willingly, your honor," called the barber, eagerly setting across the yard, smiling and simpering for all he was worth, and trying to bow ingratiatingly even as he ran.

So shaken had he been by the grim sight in the stable that it was only now Sebastian realized the barber would unfailingly discover the slight figure in boy's garments to be no boy whatever.

"Never heed, never heed!" Sebastian shouted, waving to the fellow to keep his distance, and as anxious now to stay clear of him as he had earlier been to call for his help.

But the barber, overjoyed at such unexpected business, was not so easily put off. In his fawning fashion, he set his case on the ground and peered at Isabel.

"A phlogistical subluxation, your honor," he remarked, licking his lips with much satisfaction, "easily remedied in no time at all."

"There's no need!" Sebastian cried. "My thanks and be off!"

The barber, meantime, had pulled a long, thin-bladed instrument from his case. "Have no fear, your worship. There's no pain whatever; none at all, I assure you, a mere sanguineous evacuation. Yet isn't it curious, your honor, how many are distressed at the sight?"

Now altogether at a loss, Sebastian made to strike the fellow's hand away. The barber looked at him askance and clicked his tongue.

"Ah, ah, your worship! To my eyes, your worship himself suffers from a lymphatic obstruction of the cerebellum. Allow me, your honor." So saying, he brought up his lancet in one hand and with the other quickly fastened a surprisingly firm grip on Sebastian's neck.

With a horrified protest, Sebastian flung himself aside. The determined barber, however, never loosened his hold and next thing the two were scuffling and struggling in a fashion most unseemly for doctor and patient.

Just then the wagon halted beside Sebastian. Nicholas leaped down and with astonishing agility aimed a sharp blow at the barber's head, snatched up the Princess, and heaved her unroyally to the floorboards. Next he collared Sebastian, hoisted him up in turn, with a hard knee to the seat of his breeches to hurry him along, and slapped the reins on the horse's back.

In another instant, with Sebastian hanging on for dear life, and Presto beside him, the cart went rattling at top speed through the innyard.

The barber clutched at the side of the careening vehicle, but the onrush spun him away. Nicholas, like a cherub turned coachman, urged on the straining horse, and the wagon clattered out of the sleeping town, heading for the open road.

Only when the winded horse began to slow its pace did Sebastian catch his breath and collect his wits. Nicholas had regained his customary look of innocence and appeared surprised to find himself driving a cart down an empty lane in the middle of the night. He turned to Sebastian and said:

"You're lucky you weren't shaved closer. The innkeeper warned me about that barber. A barber? One of the Regent's bloodhounds! And I daresay he's been trailing the Princess ever since she left the Glorietta. The innkeeper suspected something deep was amiss, and had his throat cut in consequence."

Sebastian felt too shaken to reply. The innkeeper's livid face and the barber's keen lancet still floated in his mind. Had it not been for Nicholas, he and the Princess both would be sprawled dead on the innyard cobbles. At this thought, he began shuddering as violently as if he had caught the ague. Even Presto, who had climbed onto Sebastian's knees, did nothing to settle his master's spirits.

At daybreak, Nicholas drove the cart off the road and reined up some way into the undergrowth. Isabel, who had been silent until now, sat up and glanced around her. The girl's face was pale, her clothing rumpled and covered with straw from the bottom of the cart, and she appeared the most miserable urchin in Hamelin-Loring rather than its Princess. Nevertheless, when she climbed to the ground, stood upright, and began to speak, Sebastian realized she had lost nothing of her regal bearing.

"Now, sir," the Princess began, "you shall apprise us of your intentions regarding the violent demise of one of our subjects. Felony unpunished, as our Minister of Justice constantly emphasized to us, results in an inevitable laxity of general behavior, with unfortunate consequences not only for the transgressors but more so for the objects of the malefaction."

Sebastian blinked at her, and burst out: "Princess Isabel, have you taken leave of your wits? The law's not on your side now! If any constable in Hamelin-Loring recognizes you, why, you'll be hustled back to the Glorietta before you can take another breath. We know who killed the innkeeper: one of Grinssorg's bloodhounds, who's likely at your heels this moment. That false barber— he'd have cut your throat in a trice, and mine too, if Nicholas hadn't saved us."

Isabel hesitated. Nicholas, who had been carefully listening to all this, quickly put in:

"I admire your concern, Your Grace, but my friend is right. The law's the last place you can turn to. And in the way of practical matters, if you don't mean to draw every eye in the Principality you'd best not go about in those clothes. The shirt will pass muster but never those breeches and jacket. If Your Grace will be so kind as to give them to me, I'll do what I can."

Isabel's chin shot up, she flushed and stared icily at Nicholas, then opened her mouth to deliver a stern reprimand.

Thinking better of it, she stayed silent; then, looking neither right nor left, she strode into the concealment of the bushes. After several moments, her jacket and breeches came flying through the air, landing at Sebastian's feet.

Nicholas plumped himself down, crossed his legs, and began ripping at the seams, stitching here and there with needle and thread from his inexhaustible pack. One blade of his pocket knife proved to be a pair of tiny scissors that he wielded so deftly Sebastian's eyes could scarcely follow.

But Sebastian was too agitated to wonder how, in addition to being cook and piper, the little man seemed as comfortable at this new trade as if he had been a tailor from the day of his birth.

"What a hornet's nest!" exclaimed Sebastian. "I promised her my help, and so she'll have it. But what can we do?"

Nicholas puffed out his cheeks and sighed unhappily. "It's not so much what we can do as what her enemies can do. The Regent's bloodhounds won't stop at killing Princess Isabel. Anyone who tries to help her—" He frowned as the scissors made an ugly snipping sound through the cloth.

"Then I've put you in the stew as well as myself," Sebastian said. "You did me a good turn and I've done you a bad one. But what other course? Nicholas, if you take the horse and wagon, you've still a chance to jump out of this pretty kettle of fish. As for me—I can't think one step beyond the next. The Princess must reach her uncle's court, her life hangs on it. But how?"

Sebastian began pacing back and forth. "Ah, Nicholas, after Baron Purn-Hessel sent me packing, I never thought I'd put myself out for the nobility—not to mention a Princess. And what a Princess! How she does go on! Her tongue's wound up tighter than a clock's mainspring! Why, she talks like a crowd! We! Us! Ours! I think the sky could fall and she'd rattle on about Councillor Hoity-Toity's opinion of cats and dogs! All the while looking as if butter wouldn't melt in her mouth! Princess Isabel? I should call her Princess Priss-and-Prim!"

Nicholas, busy plying his needle, did not reply. At last, he bit off the thread and handed the garments to Sebastian, who tossed them over the bushes.

Soon after, the Princess reappeared. Nicholas had done his work well, for the jacket and breeches fitted the girl handsomely. Isabel had also bound her dark hair closely about her head, and Sebastian was quick to admit she made a very creditable and presentable boy.

"Nicholas, you surprise me more and more," he exclaimed. "If I didn't know better, I'd swear she was a lad. Isabel? I'd say, rather, Charles, Thomas, Michael—"

"Whatever the circumstances," said the Princess, turning her green eyes on Sebastian in a cool glance, "be apprised we shall not countenance reference to ourselves under the appellation Priss-and-Prim."

Sebastian choked and turned crimson. "Princess she may be," he muttered to himself, "but she eavesdrops as well as any chambermaid."

"As for danger to our person," the Princess went on, "we have accepted this as concomitant to the duties we owe our devoted subjects. This is an obligation of nobility and, naturally, we do not expect commoners to take similar risks on our behalf."

"What!" cried Sebastian, a little vexed at this last. "Do you think a noble title makes a man brave? Now, Princess, we mean to help you because you need it, not because of your rank or ours."

Before he could say more, Presto's ears pricked up and the cat sprang to the wagon seat, where he crouched and lashed his tail. An instant later, Sebastian heard stirrings through the underbrush. The face of the Princess tensed. Nicholas flicked out the largest blade of his pocket knife.

A man stepped from the thicket, and behind him Sebastian glimpsed half-a-dozen others. It was Andreas, the road mender, and his comrades.

Sebastian heaved a sigh of relief and called out:

"Well, now, friend, if you're looking for potholes to fill, you're out of your way."

"Seek potholes?" replied Andreas, with a bitter laugh. "No more of those, my lad. Nor grapevines, either. Soon after you parted we had word the bailiff seized our homes, fields, and all, telling us there's a new law that says if a man's holdings are untenanted the Crown has a right to take them for itself!"

"Untenanted!" one of the others burst out. "Yes, that they were—and because we were obeying another of the Regent's laws! We obey one law—and another punishes us for it! Meantime, the Regent lines his pockets all the more!"

"If such is the case," Isabel began, "the Provincial Court of Justice will redress—"

"Court? Justice?" Andreas cried angrily. "For the likes of us? Tell me a better nursery tale! No, I've had my fill. I'm off to join the Captain, and so are the rest of us. Wherever he is, we'll find him." He looked sharply at Isabel. "But you, tadpole, I don't remember you along with these other two. And I've not seen you in these parts."

"A runaway apprentice," Sebastian put in hastily. "Poor devil, his master so ill-treated him he could stand it no more and took to his heels."

"Then I hope you've a swift pair of them," Andreas told Isabel, in a friendlier tone. "Run off, did you? That's a hanging crime, boy. You should know that. But no matter. You'll be safer with us than tramping the roads. Indeed, we'd welcome a minnow like you to help us cook and launder. That's no worse than whatever your trade was, and you'll get no ill treatment, for we're all good fellows here."

Isabel opened her mouth to answer, but Andreas gave the girl such a clap on the shoulder that it knocked the breath out of her.

"Better take your chances with us than play touch and go with the hangman," declared Andreas. "We'll find the Captain sooner or later. And if you're lucky, he might have a place for you with the rest of his bold band."

For once Isabel appeared at a loss what to say. Sebastian hastily stepped between the Princess and the road mender.

"All of us would take it as an honor to follow the Captain, but—but this poor lad's neither strong in the arm nor quick in the wits. So we'll make our own way as best we can, many thanks to you."

"And which way might that be?" asked Andreas, glancing kindly at the weak and dull-witted apprentice, who was clever enough to hang her head and hold her tongue.

"Why, that would be northward, sir," Nicholas put in, drawing the road mender aside before he could study Isabel too closely. "Directly northward from here, in point of fact as well as point of compass."

"Well enough," said Andreas. "We'll go northward, too, for no one knows where the Captain may show himself, and north is as good as any. And if we don't find him, sooner or later he'll find us."

Sebastian gave a puzzled, uneasy glance at Nicholas, who returned it with a faint shake of his head; the road menders had clearly made up their minds they would all travel together. At the same time, Nicholas replied to Andreas:

"No doubt he will, sir. As I've heard it told, he seeks brave fellows, and what he seeks he always finds."

Though Sebastian himself had been eager to join the Captain, he now feared this would put Isabel in a worse pickle than before. Still, since Andreas judged the question settled, he could only fall in with the plan. At least, he thought, there was more safety in numbers; and as long as the Princess managed to curb her tongue, he hoped it would somehow turn out well.

They headed northward, Nicholas driving the wagon along byways and hedgerows while the road menders held to the fields, keeping always in sight of the jolting vehicle.

Isabel, weary-eyed, sat bolt upright in a corner of the wagon. When Sebastian urged her to sleep, the Princess replied:

"We are not in a state of fatigue. As our Court Metaphysician explained clearly, such a condition is merely a figment of the imagination, and it can be overcome by disregarding the delusions of our baser natures and contemplating the higher verities."

Sebastian laughed. "I daresay the Court Metaphysician sleeps soundly in his own bed—and very likely snores, too."

The Princess gasped and looked scandalized at the notion of a snoring metaphysician. She made no move to follow the advice of Sebastian or the example of Presto, who had curled comfortably on the straw. After a little while, Nicholas halted the wagon in answer to a signal from the road menders, who had decided to stop for their afternoon meal.

"Fall to," called Andreas, as one of his fellows set a small stewpot to bubbling over a fire of twigs. "There's not much for any of us, but it will have to do for all."

Sebastian very willingly and Isabel very reluctantly accepted this offer. From his amazing pack, Nicholas pulled out provisions that more than eked out the road menders' meager supplies. When all had finished, Andreas handed the Princess the empty pot and shouted as if she were deaf as well as dull-witted:

"Here, you poor fellow, you may be good for little else but you can oblige your elders in this much. Scrape it well. Wash it clean. There, in the stream you see."

Isabel had no time to reply, for Andreas gave her a good-natured shove to set her in the proper direction. Sebastian, terrified the Princess would come out with one of her customary declamations, hustled her along, calling out:

"I'll go with the lad and see he does his work as he should."

By the streamside, he was tempted to let the Princess struggle with the pot; but the girl looked so pitifully baffled that he reached for it himself.

However, instead of gratefully handing it over to him, the Princess drew back and declared:

"Since you have chosen to present us as an individual not in full possession of his intellectual faculties, these unfortunate refurbishers of highways would regard it with suspicion if one of such a low degree of intelligence refrained from the performance of a presumably customary occupation."

Isabel, examining the greasy pot with much distaste and displeasure, began scrubbing and scraping as best she could.

"We recognize, in any event," she added, "that you demonstrated a certain presence of mind in a situation already fraught with difficulties. We trust that you will evince equal ingenuity in separating ourselves from this present company whose grievances, though eminently justifiable, have caused them to follow a course of deplorable illegality."

"What, do you call them outlaws because they seek the Captain?" Sebastian returned.

"The exploits of this despicable Captain are not entirely unknown to us in the Glorietta," said Isabel. "The Regent's Minister of State has advised us concerning him, and expressed most forcefully to us that he is our sworn enemy, a ruthless, ill-favored antagonist and no more honorable than a common brigand."

"Common brigand!" Sebastian exclaimed. "Princess Isabel, the Minister of State tells you what the Regent wants you to be told. The Captain's the only fellow to stand for justice in all the Principality. Even a fiddler has sense enough to see that!"

Isabel had turned away, finding further discussion of the Captain as distasteful as her present occupation. But hearing Sebastian's last remark, she looked at him with new interest.

"Do you imply, sir, that you perform upon the violin?"

"That I do," Sebastian answered. "Or—that I did, for

I've neither fiddle nor place, thanks to one of your own courtiers."

He told the Princess what had happened to him on account of The Purse's breeches.

But a smile never crossed Isabel's lips as she said: "While unquestionably the Royal Treasurer lacks the probity desirable in one whose position requires unassailable integrity, he is in fact a Count and designating him The Purse derogates the respect to which his rank, if nothing else, entitles him. Nonetheless, we are personally distressed that a capable musician should be without proper employment of his skill.

"We ourselves are most partial to music, though we seldom have opportunity to hear it. The Regent abominates music and tolerates none in the Glorietta unless a state occasion demands the presence of the court orchestra." She glanced shyly at Sebastian, and spoke very quietly and quickly, with considerably more warmth than usual.

"While our parents were still alive, the Glorietta was filled with music and, during our childhood, it was our pleasure to enjoy it continually. The Regent, however, has terminated all private musical performances and forbidden us to study any musical instrument even for our edification. You, sir, are fortunate in the choice of an occupation of such inherent gratification."

"Choice?" replied Sebastian. "Did I choose fiddling? I'd say it was the other way round, and fiddling chose me. For I was born to it, just as you were born to be a Princess. I assure you I wasn't consulted in the matter."

"Nor were we," Isabel murmured. "But we have often imagined the pleasures and satisfactions of being sur-

rounded by such magnificent melodiousness and partici-
pating in its production."

Sebastian was surprised at the royal interest in music,
and all the more astonished at the fondness and wistful-
ness in Isabel's voice. He shrugged, and shook his head.
"It may be pleasure for the listeners; but for the musicians it's work no different from any other. And notes are
notes, no matter who plays them."

Isabel frowned, perplexed. "Do you believe so? It
seems to us there should be considerably more to music
than merely producing the correct sounds."

"True enough," Sebastian replied. "But there, Princess, you're speaking of a true musician, who really
knows the sense of what he's playing. That's a different
matter from a simple knack for fiddling, and, indeed, one
I know nothing about."

Isabel, meantime, had finished scrubbing the pot, and
had not done too badly at it. Still pondering the girl's unexpected questions, Sebastian walked back with her to
the wagon and the waiting road menders. Andreas had
decided to press farther, and his comrades were prepar-
ing to do so.

But the face of Nicholas puckered with concern. He
had been keeping an eye on the road, and now called out
a warning.

Sebastian, too, caught sight of a patrol of soldiers
marching toward them. He quickly helped Isabel into
the cart. Before Nicholas could join them, the officer, on
a black horse, spurred his mount and galloped up to bar
their way.

"Stand fast and name yourselves!" he commanded.

"There's been foul play at Darmstel, a man murdered and a wagon stolen."

"Now, sir, you're not accusing us of such a deed?" said Nicholas in his most innocent manner.

"Don't speak of foul play when the Regent's brave scoundrels rob more than they guard," Andreas put in hotly.

"Hold your tongue," snapped the officer, as his patrol drew up behind him. "You look all a pack of villains to me. You're under arrest, the lot of you."

XII ✦ How Sebastian Tried to Make the Princess Laugh

ONE of the road menders angrily raised his mattock. Without an instant's hesitation to determine whether the man was merely threatening or meant indeed to attack him, the officer pulled a pistol from his belt and fired. The road mender clutched his breast and fell. Isabel screamed as the soldiers moved forward. Nicholas, with amazing speed, seized the officer's stirrup and flung him from the saddle.

Sebastian, jumping to his feet, was about to clamber down, but Nicholas turned quickly, slapped the horse's flank, and sent the wagon plunging through the patrol and Sebastian toppling backward onto the floorboards.

Presto bristled and yowled with alarm as the frightened horse dashed off at full gallop. The vehicle bounced and slewed from one shoulder of the road to another, while Isabel clung to the side and Sebastian tried vainly to catch the trailing reins.

Instead of slackening its gait, the animal galloped faster. Nicholas and the embattled road menders were quickly out of sight. Try as he would, Sebastian could neither halt nor slow the onrushing wagon. Seizing his green bag, he thrust it into Isabel's arms, hoping it would cushion her fall; then, as the wagon careened madly around a bend in the road, he picked up the terrified Princess, pitched her over the side, and went tumbling after. Rolling headlong into a ditch, he came to a halt, half stunned, the wind knocked out of him, and sure every bone in his body had shattered.

Presto, leaping clear at the same time, had landed on his feet. The white cat bounded ahead as Sebastian crawled from the ditch and looked about for Isabel.

The Princess was sitting in the weeds, her face in her hands. He ran to the girl and knelt beside her, asking urgently if she had been hurt. Isabel shook her head.

"The innkeeper, now the road mender," she murmured, half in tears. "We can stand no more of seeing men die. And your friend . . . the others . . . what will happen to them?"

Sebastian frowned and shook his head. "If Nicholas is as clever as I know him to be, he'll find his way out of any scrape." His words carried little conviction to Isabel and none at all to himself. Nicholas had befriended him, saved his life, and shown himself altogether stouthearted; but whether wits and courage would be enough in this instance, Sebastian dared not guess. "Come," he said, "one way or another, you can't stay here."

Uncertain whether to go looking for the wagon first, or to set out on foot in search of Nicholas, Sebastian did neither. Presto, none the worse for his wild ride, had darted into the weeds. Trying to catch him, and reproaching him for playing hide-and-seek now of all times, Sebastian caught sight of a farmhouse a little distance across the field.

The Princess was shaking so badly and had turned so pale that Sebastian knew he must find some rest and comfort for her. He beckoned to the girl, who trudged after him, her head lowered, unusually downcast and subdued.

His choice proved lucky, for the sky had begun to thicken, and the first raindrops were pattering into the dust by the time the fugitives reached the farmyard. Sebastian hurried to the building; but instead of the hospitality he hoped for, he found the house only a deserted shell and saw nothing but crumbling walls propping up a sagging roof. Presto scurried through the doorway.

"Small comfort's better than none," Sebastian said, helping the girl over the threshold. Isabel glanced around uneasily at the empty room and dead hearth, and gingerly sat down on the floor by the cheerless fireplace.

"We trust our stay will be of minimal duration," she said. "Much as we deplore the events which have brought us to our present situation, personal sensibilities must not influence our intentions, of which you are already aware."

"Do you still mean to reach Upper Cassel?" Sebastian replied, with some doubt. In the abandoned farmhouse, with the rain bucketing down, Isabel's plan seemed more foolhardy than it had at the Golden Stag. "If you must keep the Regent from the throne," he added, "I'm beginning to think we might find a better way."

"Nothing less than force of arms will suffice," replied the Princess. "Count Grinssorg is undefeatable by any other means. Even before his regency, many of the court ministers opposed him. Though nothing could be proved of Count Grinssorg's hand in it, one by one they forfeited their lives—a fall from a horse, an attack by highwaymen —and their offices were dispensed to creatures under his influence. Even so much as a whisper against him was attended by fatal consequences."

Isabel's voice faltered. "Our own beloved parents, Prince Theodore and Princess Charlotte, came to their unhappy demise through what was accounted a carriage accident. Count Grinssorg, by custom, should have been in attendance. That day, he did not accompany them, and his life was spared. The Court Metaphysician deemed it an act of providence."

"Act of providence?" exclaimed Sebastian. "Say, rather, Grinssorg had your parents murdered in cold blood! Court Metaphysician? He's no more than a puppet on a string! You can be sure the Regent has his spies and toadies among all the councillors and ministers in the Glorietta. He's no man, but a monster. And if he's taken such power into his hands, even if Prince Frederick sent an army into Hamelin-Loring, do you think it would have a chance against him? A villain like that? He'd have so many schemes, secrets, and strategies, you'd be beaten before you started."

"Our decision," replied Isabel, "is nevertheless taken."

Having declared these bold words, the Princess looked suddenly forlorn and utterly wretched. Her lips trembled, and she quickly turned her face away.

Seeing Isabel's distress, Sebastian gently put a hand on her shoulder. "Take heart, we'll find some way or other." He grinned at her. "Alas that I don't have my fiddle, for that would put you in better spirits. You talk of musicians? Whatever else they may be, they're carefree enough among themselves. Why, once we glued the First

Fiddle's music together. Ah, ah, you should have seen his face when he tried to turn his page! And I remember a day the Second Flute put soap on my bow. And I— scraping away as hard as I could, without a sound, wondering if I'd gone deaf that instant!"

Sebastian went from one tale to another, making each more comical than the last, and even inventing the most preposterous escapades and adventures, trying as well as he could to cheer the unhappy Isabel.

The Princess listened with interest, but with an altogether solemn, sobersided expression on her face. Admitting that her plight gave her no cause for mirth, Sebastian began to suspect that laughter was not one of the royal characteristics.

He fell silent then. His jesting, which he had hoped would brighten his own spirits as well as Isabel's, only left him the more downcast and uncertain. Presto, meanwhile, finishing his close inspection of the room, padded to the fireplace and, without invitation, hopped onto the royal knees. Instead of reprimanding the cat for his impertinence, Isabel cautiously stroked him. In answer, Presto began purring as loudly as he could. In a few moments, disregarding the remarks of the Court Metaphysician, Isabel gave way to her exhaustion; her eyes closed, her head dropped back against the stones of the fireplace, and she was soon fast asleep.

Sebastian put his head in his hands. His thoughts turned again to Nicholas, realizing how much he had counted on his friend's help, and wondering what, if anything, he could hope to do unaided. To seek Nicholas would only bring the Princess into greater danger. As for the Captain, whom she considered her sworn enemy, to come upon him now, even by accident, might be still worse. To strike across country and make their way northward on foot appeared Isabel's only chance, yet the rashest plan of all.

So he went on, back and forth, betwixt and between, until he could puzzle it out no longer and, in spite of himself, sank into a corner and slept fitfully. Even then his dreams gave him less relief than his waking thoughts, and he started up in terror.

It was nearly daybreak and he had been roused not by his nightmare but by a noise outside. He jumped to his feet. The Princess, half dazed, sat up as Presto sprang to the ledge above the fireplace. Sebastian could see nothing through the shutters, but the latch began rattling loudly.

Hopeful it was Nicholas, terrified it might be the murderous barber, Sebastian cried "Who's there?" and at the same time flung himself against the door.

No answer came. Though he pushed with all his might, the door was forced little by little ajar until finally it burst open and sent him stumbling back into the room.

In the doorway stood a huge black bear.

XIII ⟐ How Sebastian
Danced with a Bear

SEBASTIAN flung up his hands to fend off the oncoming animal, which was a good two heads taller and three times heavier than himself, and shouted for Isabel to run clear of the house. The bear straightened on its hind legs, caught Sebastian's fist in one great paw, and with the other clapped him about the waist.

Sure his last moments had come, Sebastian fought with all his strength. Tightening its grip, however, the bear led the struggling Sebastian in a ponderous dance, shuffling across the floor, turning right and left, holding its unwilling partner in a harmless but inescapable grasp.

Next instant, as the bear quickened the measure, Sebastian glimpsed four human legs, feet pointed at the ceiling, kicking and twirling about the room. First thinking the shock of being seized by the lumbering animal had truly driven him out of his wits, he finally realized the legs belonged to a pair of gaily clad young men dancing on their hands: an observation that only added to his bewilderment, as did the sudden appearance of a tall, red-caped figure, who clapped his hands sharply and whistled piercingly through his teeth.

At this, the two fellows righted themselves with a nimble somersault. The bear left off dancing, loosened his hold, and bowed solemnly, gazing at Sebastian with a pair of sad brown eyes.

The new arrival clapped his hands again. Sebastian, still trying to catch his breath, saw him to be a florid-faced man with an enormous hawk nose, dark eyes under bushy brows, and a black, bristling mustache so long that its tips nearly twined about his ears. At a rakish angle on top of his billowing white wig sat a three-cornered hat bedecked with trailing yellow plumes. Sweeping off this headpiece, he bowed grandly and cried in a ringing voice:

"Quicksilver's Gallimaufry-Theatricus greets you! Adam, the famous dancing bear! His superb trainer, Winkler! The world-renowned, inimitable, one and only Flasch, scintillating star of our company!

"And I, Quicksilver in person, manager and director," he went on, throwing back his cape to show a bright purple waistcoat with orange facings, brass buttons, and close-fitting breeches. "And last, though by no means least, known and admired in every corner of Hamelin-Loring, that flower of delight, the beauteous Thornless Rose herself, Madame Sophie!"

Brandishing his plumed hat, Quicksilver stepped aside as a plump woman curtseyed in the doorway. To Sebastian's eye, the Thornless Rose was by no means in her first bloom, and the tight lacings of her fancy bodice threatened to give way at any moment. Despite Quicksilver's claims, Sebastian had never heard of Madame Sophie or any of the troupe; or for that matter, the Gallimaufry-Theatricus.

"And now," continued Quicksilver, "in exchange for a simple repast and a ducat or so to put us in spirits, you'll see with no more effort than opening your eyes what thousands have journeyed leagues to witness—"

"Master Quicksilver," Sebastian put in, before the director of the Gallimaufry-Theatricus could speak further, "we're only travelers taking shelter. The house has no more ducats in it than it has owners."

"Eh?" said Quicksilver. "Neither meat nor money?"

Flasch and Winkler, who had begun doing handsprings, left off immediately. The Thornless Rose rolled up her eyes in dismay; and Quicksilver, disgusted, tossed his hat in the corner.

"I should have known," he sighed, "there's been only bad luck and empty pockets since my two best players were arrested. Well, so much for that." He turned to the Thornless Rose.

"No sense lingering, my honeyduck. Off and away! What we'll do to flesh out our program, I've no idea— unless it's fire-eating and sword-swallowing."

"And that it shan't be," replied the Thornless Rose in a prickly tone altogether contrary to her name. "Ah, no, Quicksilver, I'll have no more of that. You'll not sweet-talk me into swallowing those greasy sabers and foul-smelling torches, and swear to me it's good for my complexion! I can taste them yet!"

"Little wife of my heart!" Quicksilver exclaimed. "Dearest flower of my life! If it's not to your liking, I wouldn't dream of even considering it!" He gave the stout lady a very arch glance, and gallantly twirled his mustache:

"Though you do cut a handsome figure in spangles,

and it would be a crime and shame to deprive the audience of your charms."

He chucked the portly Rose under her ample chin. Though Madame Sophie at first had given every sign that she was familiar with Quicksilver's methods of persuasion, she now seemed on the verge of giving in to the scheme, as the impresario continued to pile compliment on top of compliment, and all such transparent flattery that Sebastian wondered how she could possibly believe a single word of it. Only when Quicksilver ran out of endearing terms did Madame Sophie regain her resolution and adamantly shake her head.

"Ah well," sighed Quicksilver, "perhaps we'll try 'The Amazon Queen' again. It should do well enough for the bumpkins in the north, since they dote on anything with horses in it. Adam shall ride one, and you the other, as you do so delightfully—"

Isabel had kept apart from the confusion wrought by the troupe, but now she hurried over to Quicksilver and said:

"Sir, do your remarks imply the direction of your progress to be northward?"

"Hey, ho, what fellow's this?" asked Quicksilver. "He's got a pair of sharp ears and a glib tongue."

"Pay him no heed," Sebastian said hastily. "It's only Charles—ah, my servant."

"Servant?" said Quicksilver. "You travel in fine style, one vagabond to serve another! But indeed, to answer the question: the Gallimaufry-Theatricus, yielding to the demands of its impatient public, undertakes a journey to the most distant reaches of the Principality, no town too large, no hamlet too small, with its entire cast—ah, what's left of it—with new settings, most artfully contrived—"

"Well, then, Master Quicksilver," Sebastian put in, his mind working as fast as it could, trying to weigh one course against the other, his concern for Nicholas and the safety of Isabel, and the chance of the barber being at his heels. "We, too, are going in that direction, and you might find some profit in it if you let us join you."

"The two of you?" replied Quicksilver, looking doubtful. "It's true, we're a little shorthanded. My Harlequin and Columbine made the disastrous mistake of incorporating in their last performance a jest or two at the Regent's expense. The audience was overjoyed, but within the hour a pair of constables had them in fetters. And what's become of them—" A grim shadow passed over the impresario's face, but in another moment he returned to his flamboyant bearing.

"New talent is the lifeblood of the Theatricus," he declared grandly, then added, out of the side of his mustache, "Do you have any? In short, what can you do?" He glanced at Presto, still perched on the ledge. "Is that magnificent creature yours? Can it do tricks? Jump through a fiery hoop?"

"Better than that," Sebastian answered; and, taking Quicksilver's own attitude as a clue, he boldly declared, "You'll have the finest fiddler in Hamelin-Loring."

"The cat plays the fiddle?" exclaimed Quicksilver. "Marvelous! Magnificent! He's hired. We'll make up some posters directly."

"Not my cat," Sebastian said. "I mean myself."

"Oh?" Quicksilver replied, with disappointment. He thought for a moment. "I'd rather show a performing cat.

Even so, there might be a place in the Theatricus for a fiddler."

"Most certainly there is," put in Madame Sophie. "If he can scrape any sort of tune, better his fiddling than my fire-eating."

"Very well, my lad," Quicksilver said. "Let's hear you play."

"My fiddle," Sebastian began, "I have none—"

Quicksilver frowned. "No fiddle? Ah, that won't do at all. I've worked more than one hoax on the audience— dazzled them with mirrors to make our troupe look twice its size, dressed up mackerels and called them mermaids. . . . But a fiddler without a fiddle? They'll never swallow that."

Madame Sophie took her husband's arm and spoke apart with him for a moment. Quicksilver's face brightened as he turned back to Sebastian.

"As Madame Sophie, that pearl of femininity, that jewel beyond price, has so charmingly pointed out, the Gallimaufry-Theatricus presently lacks a clown. You'll have the part, if you like. As for your lackey, we'll find something useful."

"But I know nothing of that," Sebastian said. "I'm a fiddler."

"Fiddler, clown, it's all one at bottom," replied Quicksilver. "Come along. We'll have you fitted out in no time."

FLASCH, Winkler, and Adam, seeing no chance to turn a ducat, had already gone. Madame Sophie and Quicksilver followed, and as soon as they were out the door, Princess Isabel spoke quickly to Sebastian.

"Although we deplore your present choice of occupation for us as much as we regretted your previous one, we nevertheless desire to express appreciation for your service on our behalf."

Sebastian shook his head doubtfully. "Thank me later, if you've still a mind to do so, after we see what this flock of odd birds has in store for us. The world-famous Gallimaufry-Theatricus? Well, whatever it may be, it's our best chance so far—and for that matter, our only one."

Quicksilver was calling him. Picking up his bag, and with Presto padding after, Sebastian stepped into the yard to see a pair of gaudily painted wagons, one open-topped, the other long and sausage-shaped with a canvas cover over the curving wooden ribs. The impresario had climbed through a rear entry into the latter vehicle, which looked like a cross between a tent on wheels and a ship whose sails had collapsed.

Sebastian was about to follow when he heard an angry voice behind him. He turned and saw the tumbler, the acclaimed star of the Theatricus, seize Isabel by the scruff of the neck and give her a tooth-rattling shake.

"I'll swallow none of your sauce, you little villain!" cried Flasch. "When I tell you to lend a hand with the wagon, you'll do as I say without fancy back talk."

Alarmed that the Princess might have betrayed herself, but angrier at seeing the girl mistreated, Sebastian hurried protectively to Isabel's side.

The tumbler, whose tight, arrogant face was set off by shining dark ringlets, let go of the Princess and turned a scornful glance on Sebastian.

"Fiddler, your lackey needs a lesson in manners."

"If that's so, you're not the one to teach it," Sebastian replied, setting Isabel behind him. "Lay hands on him again and you'll learn your own manners from me."

"Hoo, hoo!" cried Flasch in a great show of mock terror. "We've a fighting cock as well as a fiddler. But I doubt your spurs are as sharp as your tongue." So saying, he reached out and gave Sebastian a smart fillip on the end of his nose. "There! Tune your fiddle to that!"

With a cry of pain and indignation, Sebastian shot out a fist that would have laid the star performer low had Flasch been there to receive it. But the tumbler, in a trice, turned a somersault, flipped upside down in the air and, with a flying foot, gave him such a kick to the side of the head that Sebastian went spinning.

"*Hop-la!*" cried Flasch, striking an acrobat's pose. "Will you dance another measure?"

Despite the tumbler's .agility, Sebastian was furious enough to risk another set-to, and would have flung himself bodily on the grinning Flasch had not Quicksilver hurried out to separate the opponents.

"A high-spirited performance," laughed Quicksilver, clapping Sebastian on the back. "But you're out of your role. Come now, we've a matter to settle."

Still smarting, Sebastian followed the impresario into the van. Once there, however, he forgot his singing head and bruised face and cried out in astonishment. From the wooden ribs hung the most mixed array of spangled costumes, swords, spears, wigs, and masks; on the floor, pots of paint, and a chest overflowing with a king's ransom in precious gems and glittering crowns—though, looking closer, he saw they were only glass and pasteboard. Presto, always curious, lost no time in exploring this hodgepodge.

"I see the spectacular Flasch has signed his name on you," said Quicksilver, peering at Sebastian's face, where the bruise from the tumbler's nimble toe had begun turning greenish-purple and was throbbing painfully. "Pay him no mind. It's only temperament, my boy, temperament: the curse of our profession. We'll see to it this very moment."

Dipping a small brush into a jar filled with pinkish paste, Quicksilver daubed away at Sebastian's bruise so cleverly there was soon no trace of it whatever. "There!" he cried. "Good as new."

"So it looks," replied Sebastian, "but it feels no better than it did."

"Why, of course it doesn't," said Quicksilver. "Did you expect it to? That's not the way of it at all. Appearance, my boy! Appearance! That's what counts in the Gallimaufry-Theatricus—and elsewhere, too, I'll be bound. Now, then, for your costume, you shall have the one poor Lelio used."

"Whoever Lelio is," replied Sebastian, who had begun to feel that Quicksilver was pressing and hustling him along with no chance to reflect, "I still have to tell you, in all honesty, that music's my trade, not mummery."

"Nonsense!" declared Quicksilver. "As for mummery and miming, who's not a player one way or the other? Indeed, my boy, how else can you be whatever you choose? A king one night, a clown the next! A thousand different roles one after the other!"

So saying, he picked up one of the pasteboard crowns from the chest, clapped it onto Sebastian's head, and followed this with a series of false noses in wax—long ones, short ones, turned up and turned down—which he put over Sebastian's real one; and pulled off again in such rapid succession that Sebastian, glimpsing his changing face in a looking glass, burst out laughing at the sight.

"Ah, ah, Quicksilver!" he cried. "I hardly know myself! So be it, I'll play whatever part you want, though it's all make-believe and moonshine."

"Make-believe and moonshine?" exclaimed Quicksilver. He grinned and winked at Sebastian, and lowered his voice to a whisper. "To be sure it is. The crowds know it as well as the players do, but love it nonetheless. Indeed, they thrive on it! If a man's got no meat in his belly, what else can he swallow but moonshine? I know this well, my lad, for I was a boy in the gutters of Loringhold; and the ravishing Madame Sophie once cried fish in Loringhold Market."

A loud crash interrupted Quicksilver's discourse. Presto had been ferreting among the oddments, and the whole pile now came toppling down. The white cat sprang away to escape burial under the clutter, then darted back and, with renewed eagerness, began scrabbling at the bottom of the heap.

Sebastian bent to pick him up. "Is it a mouse, you brigand? Let the poor thing be, it's no fair match between you."

He stopped short and looked again to make sure his eyes had not tricked him.

Presto had uncovered a fiddle.

"Why, Quicksilver, you've hoaxed me better than your audience," cried Sebastian, "and had me think you'd no instrument for me."

"Nor do I," declared the impresario. "Lelio's fiddle? No, my lad, you'll want no part of that. Indeed, as Lelio told it, the thing's accursed."

"ᴀᴄᴄᴜʀsᴇᴅ?" Sebastian exclaimed. "Ah, Quicksilver, enough of your make-believe and moonshine! A fiddle's a fiddle! Strings and wood, no more no less. As for this one—"

He dropped to his knees and drew the violin from the pile. As he did, he caught his breath and his hands trembled. The instrument was the most beautiful he had ever seen, and made with such perfection he could not believe his eyes. The wood was dark, deeply and richly varnished, and through it ran a lighter grain, like a flame glowing of itself. On the scroll was carved a woman's face, so lovely and so lifelike it seemed about to speak. Wonderstruck, he turned to Quicksilver:

"Play games with wax noses and gems of paste if you will, but I'm a fiddler and know this for a true masterpiece."

"A splendid piece of work," the impresario agreed. "Yes, my boy, no doubt of that. Indeed, that's why I never had the heart to break it up."

"Break it?" cried Sebastian. "Why, Quicksilver, how can you speak of smashing it? That's madness!"

"It was not my wish," Quicksilver answered, "but Lelio's."

"Lelio wanted it destroyed?" Sebastian asked. "Ah, no, you're joking. No fiddler in all the world would give up such a prize once it was in his hands. Who is this fellow? Where is he now?"

"In his grave," replied Quicksilver, "a happier resting place than ever he found outside of it. Who was he? I know hardly more of him than you do, and nothing at all of where he came from. But I've never seen his like before or since. You'd split your sides laughing, beg him to stop and let you catch your breath; then beg him to keep on with his drolleries. And he, never cracking a smile—"

"But Quicksilver," Sebastian put in, "are you talking of a clown or a fiddler? Either way, how did he come by such an instrument?"

"It had been given him," Quicksilver replied. "As he told the tale, it had passed through many hands before reaching his. Clown he surely was, or pretended to be. But a fiddler, too. And what a fiddler! Ah, my boy, I've never heard such music. Magnificent! Incredible! With Lelio as violinist for the troupe, I'd have sworn our fortunes were made. But for all his clowning on the stage, he was a moody fellow and seldom played the fiddle for an audience. A great loss, my boy. To the Gallimaufry-Theatricus, to anyone who ever heard him—and even to those who never heard him at all, for they'll never know what they missed. Indeed, you can't honestly say you've truly heard music unless you've heard Lelio.

"The times I've listened to him," Quicksilver went on, "I'd swear his tunes could have melted mountains! And when he struck up a lively air, it was all you could do to keep your feet from dancing willy-nilly."

"Now, Quicksilver," Sebastian returned, "this speaks well of his playing, but says nothing at all of an accursed fiddle."

"Lelio called it so," Quicksilver answered, "and claimed each owner came to grief because of it. As he said, they weren't the ones who owned the fiddle, but it was the fiddle that owned them; and if they hoped to get music from it, it would cost them dearly. According to Lelio, one poor fellow wasted away the longer he played, as if the fiddle were drinking his life like a glass of wine. Another took leave of his wits altogether, and died a-babbling the fiddle was to blame."

"And Lelio?" Sebastian asked.

The impresario shook his head. "Why, I should say he died of sorrow."

"What, a clown and die from sorrow?" exclaimed Sebastian. "Was it such a sad thing for him to make others laugh?"

"No," replied Quicksilver, "I think his heart broke because he knew the fiddle had music in it that even he could never hope to play. He could hear it in his head, but never have it in his fingers. It ate away at him, night and day, until he sickened with brooding over it. And so the fiddle brought him to grief, too; and took his life as surely as it had all the others. He told me this as he lay dying in this very wagon, and at the end he begged me to smash the accursed thing, to break it into splinters and burn it."

Throughout this tale, Quicksilver had dropped his theatrical manner and had spoken in a whisper. His florid face and huge mustache seemed now to Sebastian only a mask the impresario had chosen for himself among the clutter of wigs and wax noses. Beneath it, Sebastian caught a quick glimpse of an unhappy urchin from the gutters of Loringhold.

"I never heeded him," Quicksilver said quietly. "The fiddle was too beautiful to be destroyed. For you see, my boy, even in the Gallimaufry-Theatricus we know the difference between a stage property and the genuine article."

Sebastian was silent for a while. He turned the violin over in his hands and gently touched the carved features, cool and smooth to his fingertips. "Then, Quicksilver, it seems to me you'd have done well to find someone else willing to play it."

The impresario shook his head. "Easier said than done. For there was one thing more that Lelio told me. The fiddle would play only in the hands of a master musician worthy of the instrument. And I believe he told the truth. From the moment he died, the fiddle lost its sound. I've tried to play it myself and so have a dozen others: street fiddlers, court musicians, music masters, whoever crossed my way; and some of them, I'll tell you, had high opinions of their skill. But the fiddle never answered them. Finally I gave up and put the thing away, for it stayed silent as a bell without a clapper."

"Then, surely, it won't play for me," Sebastian replied. "I've a little knack with a fiddle, nothing more. Worthy of such an instrument? I'd not even pretend to be. Still, I can't believe there's a fiddle made that won't give some sound or other. Voiceless? Not even a squeak or a scrape? No, Quicksilver, that's more of your moonshine."

"See for yourself," answered Quicksilver.

Sebastian took his bow from the green bag. The violin, as he tucked it under his chin, weighed no more than a feather. He drew the bow across the strings, finding them to his surprise perfectly in tune and their temper true. Suddenly, to his astonishment, he began to play, and the notes surged from the instrument in the purest tones he had ever heard. His fingers danced effortlessly up and down the fingerboard. The violin seemed to spring alive and sing in his hands.

Quicksilver's jaw dropped. Presto, who had gone back to his game among the oddments, left off and sat motionless on his haunches.

But most amazed of all was Sebastian himself. At the sound of this violin, he found himself halfway between tears and laughter, between sheer delight and a strange and sudden grief. Only with greatest reluctance did he stop.

"Ah, Quicksilver, now I know you've been joking with me," he exclaimed. "A master musician? I was Baron Purn-Hessel's Fourth Fiddle, not the leader of his orchestra. Worthy of the instrument? Why, it answers so easily it almost plays by itself! The clumsiest apprentice could make it sing! Oh, you tried to hoax me, telling me it's accursed and all such nonsense. But I've caught you at your own game!"

Quicksilver stared at him for a long moment before answering. "Think what you please," he murmured. "It plays for you as it played for no other. I've told you all I know of the thing. Do you want it? Take it."

Now doubly astonished, scarcely believing Quicksilver meant to give him this magnificent fiddle, Sebastian

could only stammer incoherent thanks. Then he turned
to Presto:

"And you, Your Exalted Catliness! My dearest Gauli-
Mauli! If it hadn't been for you—Presto, you've done me
the best of turns. You deserve a gold saucer! A silken pillow! And more! Well, you'll have them, somehow, and
there's my word on it!"

Taking the clown's costume, and clutching the violin
and bow under his arm, Sebastian hurried from the van.
Outside, the Princess was stirring a large basin of porridge and trying, with little success, to keep it from turning lumpy.

"See this!" exclaimed Sebastian. "A present from
Quicksilver! He's put a fortune, a king's ransom in my
hands! Such a stroke of luck as I've never had in all my
life!"

As he showed Isabel the violin and gave her a very
confused account of what had happened, the girl's excitement grew as great as his own.

"We request you to let us scrutinize this instrument,"
Isabel said, with uncustomary eagerness. "Yes, we agree
its external characteristics are remarkable, and apparent
even to us, although our knowledge of such musical de-
vices is unfortunately limited."

Pleased and proud to show off the splendid fiddle, Sebastian held up the instrument to point out the details of
shaping and joining, and the cleverness of its construc-
tion:

"These pegs that tighten the strings—each one shaped so perfectly. And this—the bridge. And these openings on either side—look how they curve. I've never seen them cut so beautifully."

As he went on, Sebastian's own enthusiasm surprised him. Serving Baron Purn-Hessel, he had never troubled to observe his former instrument so closely; in fact, it had made little difference to him which fiddle he played.

Now, with Lelio's violin, the more he looked the more he saw, and discovered added beauty which had gone unnoticed in Quicksilver's wagon. The back of the instrument, though made from two pieces of wood, appeared altogether seamless, even more richly varnished and polished than the front. Following the curved edges of the violin, a line of inlaying, hardly a hairsbreadth, was set with pearls so tiny that the workmanship seemed beyond the skill of any human craftsman.

Isabel was admiring the carved face. "We find it difficult to ascertain the expression on these features, inasmuch as they give us the impression of being different at each new regard."

"It's the finest carving I've ever seen," Sebastian replied, "but has nothing at all to do with the sound. Appearance may be all that counts in the Gallimaufry-Theatricus. Not with a fiddle. The voice is what matters. And this one—listen!"

He would have tried out the instrument again, then and there, but the porridge had begun to scorch. Isabel hurried to rescue it; at the same time Adam and Winkler arrived, both looking hungry as bears.

Sebastian turned away. His excitement over the gift made him forget his hunger, so instead of joining the others at the cook fire he went a little distance apart.

As he began bowing the strings, the voice of the fiddle rose even more splendidly than before. He had meant only to try a simple air; but the instrument sang a different melody, not at all of his choosing, that flowed from the violin like a shaft of sunlight. The bright weavings of sound filled his heart and drew him into a sky of blinding brilliance. The carved head had come alive, the lips moved in a wordless song whose full meaning escaped him; yet, even without words, he understood fragments of it and yearned to hear more. How long he played he could not guess, for time and place had vanished; Hamelin-Loring and the Gallimaufry-Theatricus had grown suddenly less real than the meshes of music that held him a willing captive. He stopped only when his joy seemed beyond bearing; and the silence that followed when he lowered his bow nearly made him cry out in loss.

Flasch was standing a few paces away, watching him. The tumbler gave a scornful grimace.

"Leave off that caterwauling," he said. "It's enough to split my ears and spoil my digestion." He made a curt motion with his head. "Get on with you, fiddler, if you mean to travel with us."

Sebastian, still under the spell of the music, blinked at the acrobat.

"What, are you witless as well as deaf?" said Flasch. "Get to the wagon. We'll not wait on a fiddler's pleasure." He raised a hand as Sebastian made a step forward, adding:

"Let's understand each other, once and for all. Quicksilver's taken you on against my judgment. I've no fondness for musicians, let alone a pair of ne'er-do-wells who dropped out of nowhere. If it's in your mind to make yourself a star turn in the Theatricus, then put that thought out of your head."

The tumbler's words and bearing were enough to silence the last echoes of the violin and set Sebastian's blood boiling at the sight of the arrogant Flasch. Before he could answer him in kind, even at the risk of another set-to, Quicksilver began shouting for all to hasten. Sebastian strode past the acrobat and hurried to the second wagon, where Adam hunched on the box. In back, with Presto, Isabel sat on the floorboards amid some tall, oddly shaped containers.

Sebastian sprang up beside her, forgetting his encounter with the tumbler in his eagerness to tell her more of Lelio's fiddle. "I still can't believe it," he exclaimed. "I've played music all my life, but never heard such as this. Why, it even frightens me a little. And strangest yet—" He stopped and looked at Isabel, who appeared more wretched and downcast than ever. "What's amiss? We'll soon be on our way. Quicksilver's pulled us both out of a scrape. Why, you should be laughing instead of glooming."

"Levity ill becomes a sovereign," Isabel replied, "as the Lord Chamberlain frequently emphasized to us. Furthermore, in your absence, we have been subjected to a consideration as unseemly as it is distasteful."

"That villain Flasch again!" Sebastian burst out. "Well, have no fear. I've a score to settle with him and I'll add yours to it. What's he been up to?"

Isabel shook her head. "The matter concerns the individual denominating herself the Thornless Rose. It was her suggestion to offer as an attraction the spectacle of ourselves dancing with—with that hirsute creature."

"Adam?" Sebastian exclaimed. "Madame Sophie would have you dance with a bear? Well, there's no danger. Adam's a good fellow. I've trod a measure with him, and he's gentle as a lamb."

"We find the proposition entirely unacceptable," Isabel replied. "Additionally, it was suggested that, in keeping with the common practices of the public stage, it would be appropriate for us to assume feminine attire."

"A girl disguised as a boy disguised as a girl! Well, so much the better. Unless, of course, you don't know how to dance."

"You should be made aware," Isabel declared, "that our education has included an attentive study of corporeal movements designed as a beneficial enhancement of our physical well-being."

"Then there's nothing against it," Sebastian said. "You and Adam will make a handsome couple!"

"In the first instance," Isabel returned, "we do not believe such an undertaking necessary to the conclusion of our endeavors. In the second, the costume made available to us by Madame Sophie is both scant and gaudy, two characteristics in themselves sufficing to remove it from our consideration. We find it irretrievably beneath even the lowest limit of decorum."

Sebastian looked at her in astonishment. "You mean to risk life and limb, to make your way half across Hamelin-Loring with Grinssorg's bloodhounds on your track, to raise an army—and you stick at the matter of a few spangles?"

Isabel blushed. "We have already compromised our dignity far beyond anything we had foreseen, and categorically refuse to entertain even the remotest possibility of our appearance before an assembly of spectators in attire suitable only for the eyes of our ladies-in-waiting, and even then in the strictest privacy of our chambers."

"Well, so be it," Sebastian replied. "Quicksilver's sure to find something else for you to do. Alas that you can't play an instrument, for that would answer best of all."

Isabel brightened at this. "Would you consider, then, undertaking our instruction in such an enterprise? We should be most agreeable to applying ourselves assiduously, for example, to the perfection of our ability on the violin."

"Teach you to play the fiddle overnight? Ah, Princess, I wish I could," Sebastian answered, "but I'm afraid it's a harder matter than that. But it makes no difference, for we'll not stay with the Theatricus a moment longer than we have to. With luck, you'll be in Upper Cassel before I could even teach you to hold the bow straight."

The Princess appeared surprised, seeming to have forgotten, for an instant, her goal of reaching Prince Frederick's court. Then she lowered her eyes and said, with unaccustomed hesitation:

"Presupposing a successful termination of our purpose, it would not be displeasing to us if you were to assume the capacity of instructor in music—"

At this, Sebastian laughed wholeheartedly. "Me? A court music councillor? From what I've seen of the nobility, I think we'd soon be at loggerheads. But if we ever get out of this pickle, and you get back your throne, I'm sure you can royally summon music masters by the dozen to the Glorietta."

Isabel glanced at him quickly. "We are aware of the

instructional resources ordinarily available. This was not a command but a suggestion directed to a specific individual."

Sebastian felt his own cheeks flush. "Well, it might be," he said, trying to cover his confusion. "But I've promised Presto a gold saucer and silk cushion, and that must be part of the bargain."

Isabel did not answer, for Winkler now jumped up beside Adam and slapped the reins across the haunches of the swaybacked gray horse. Flasch, in the other van, cracked his whip. The wagons of the Gallimaufry-Theatricus lurched and rattled along the muddy track, heading northward.

ISABEL said no more. Sebastian, too, was silent, holding
Presto on his knees and settling as comfortably as he
could in the back of the jolting wagon. His joy and wonder at Quicksilver's gift had begun to crumble a little
around the edges, leaving him strangely weary. The short
time he had played Lelio's fiddle had exhausted him
more than all of Baron Purn-Hessel's concerts, serenades,
cassations, and divertissements put together. "I could almost believe Quicksilver," he told Presto, who had rolled
over like a kitten, all paws in the air. "I feel as though
I've been fiddling on my own skin and bones instead of
four strings. But that's not your concern, is it, Your Catliness?"

In answer, Presto did no more than flick his whiskers.
Sebastian sighed. For a time, he had forgotten the murderous barber, the embattled road menders, and Nicholas; but these thoughts returning only filled him with
more uneasiness. Whatever safety the Gallimaufry-Theatricus offered now appeared frail. Even Quicksilver's
troupe had suffered from the Regent's tyranny and,
while the two vans bore northward at a fair pace, the

shadow of Grinssorg still seemed to lie heavily upon them.

When Quicksilver finally ordered a halt, Sebastian realized it was not so much to rest the company as it was to refurbish and repair the stage properties and assorted gear. The impresario himself had pulled out a length of heavy chain and, sitting cross-legged on the ground, busied himself hammering and filing the links.

"There," said Quicksilver, while Sebastian watched him curiously. "When I play 'The Mighty Hercules,' these should snap like matchsticks." He mixed the iron filings with a little paste and carefully daubed the cut portions of the chain. "That will do nicely. Look as close as you please, you'll never notice. Someday, I must try filling those gaps with gunpowder and find a way to set it off. Ah, my lad, now that would be a splendid effect."

Sebastian laughed in spite of himself. "Quicksilver, you're a hoaxer born, and so brazen about it I can't bring myself to think ill of you."

Quicksilver grinned. "Nor should you. Why, my boy, there's as much art in pulling off an illusion as doing it in fact—and likely more! Make-believe and moonshine? Say naught against them! Before the Regent's bloodhounds snatched away my Harlequin and Columbine, we used to put up a play that did handsomely for us. No more than a nursery tale of a swineherd who killed a dragon and married a princess—with your obedient servant as the dragon. Moonshine? On the face of it, if you will. But I'll tell you, my lad, there wasn't a plowboy or kitchenmaid, doddering grandsire or crone of eighty, who didn't see themselves as the brave swineherd or fairhaired princess. For a little time, at least. And were none the worse for it. Indeed, I'd say they were all the better! Make-believe? There's more truth at the bottom of it than you'll find in the Glorietta's Court Gazette!"

So saying, Quicksilver packed up his chain and whistled through his teeth for all to mount the wagons. Sebastian had judged that Quicksilver would continue without delay to the larger towns in the north. But he soon learned the impresario was unable to resist the prospect of any audience however small. Late in the day, Quicksilver signaled the vans to turn from the highway and he now led the Theatricus into Great Brunswick, a village of ramshackle dwellings matching its name as well as the Merry Host had matched his own.

To signal their arrival, Quicksilver climbed on top of his wagon and set to pounding a battered drum for all he was worth. Flasch and Winkler turned cartwheels around the marketplace; the Thornless Rose and Adam balanced on the swaybacked horses to the wild cheers of the onlookers, who, from all Sebastian could tell, had never seen anything like it in their lives.

Quicksilver next directed the caravan to an open field and ordered the troupe to make ready for their first performance.

"Hop, hop, lend a hand, the two of you," Quicksilver cried to Sebastian and Isabel. "Haul down those boxes! Up with the stage! Unroll the curtain!"

"Well, Quicksilver, you had me think I was to play a clown for you," Sebastian replied, overwhelmed at the amount of toil confronting him.

"So you shall, so you shall," Quicksilver answered. "In the Gallimaufry-Theatricus we double and treble ourselves. You'll be a porter as well as a player, and who knows what-all besides. To work, my boy, and you'll see there's more behind the stage than on it."

Isabel, under the direction of Madame Sophie, went about her own work. But Sebastian's labor was made more unpleasant by Flasch, who had appointed himself Sebastian's taskmaster.

"Don't think you'll keep those lily fingers of yours out of the tar pot," declared the tumbler, giving no sign he wished to patch up their quarrel. "Musicians! A sorry lot, all of you."

Sebastian soon found himself puffing and straining with his efforts, and all in all working harder than he had ever done for Baron Purn-Hessel. Yet he was fascinated to see how a wagon could be taken apart in the twinkling of an eye. The floorboards turned into a rough stage; the ribs and stakes became supports and frames for curtains; the wheels, candleholders; and the whole thing as complicated and clever as a spider web.

Even Adam had been set to work hauling planks and rolling barrels. But Presto, as Sebastian expected, curled up at the front of the platform and surveyed the doings with cool interest, as though none of it were new to him and he had seen it all before.

Winkler, meanwhile, had inflated a great red-and-yellow bag with hot air from a bonfire. The balloon swelled like a giant's plaything, bobbing and swaying in the breeze that would have carried it away if a stout rope had not moored the wicker basket to the ground.

"Magnificent!" Quicksilver exclaimed, beaming proudly at the gaudy bubble. "Ah, the crowds love it," he told the perspiring Sebastian. "For a penny, they go aloft

—scarcely higher than my head. But for all their clamor you might think they were sailing to the moon!"

By dusk, the torches were blazing. Quicksilver had dressed himself in a costume of bright feathers and looked like a cross between peacock and rooster, an effect with which he seemed inordinately delighted.

Sebastian, following the impresario's directions, donned Lelio's white, loose-fitting jacket and pantaloons and covered his face with whitewash from one of Quicksilver's paint pots.

Since Isabel still refused absolutely to do a turn on the stage, Madame Sophie had given her a tray of rather shriveled apples and oranges to be hawked among the onlookers.

Presto had not left his post on the stage. As the time for the performance drew closer, Sebastian went to pick him up and carry him behind the curtain.

Presto bristled, and growled deep in his throat. His eyes were set on the townsfolk who had begun crowding the field.

"Don't tell me Your Catliness is bashful," Sebastian said, trying to lift the struggling Presto to his shoulder.

The white cat only growled the louder, set his ears close to his head, and fixed his gaze more intently.

Sebastian glanced at the crowd. His blood ran cold and his face went paler than his chalky mask.

In the forefront of the onlookers stood the barber.

XVIII ❧ How Sebastian
Played a Tune

THE Regent's bloodhound no longer carried his black case and now wore a tradesman's smock instead of his foppish costume, but Sebastian could not mistake the man's puffy features. The false barber's eyes darted all about, scanning the faces in the audience.

Sebastian snatched up Presto and ran to find Isabel. Quicksilver at the same time hauled up the curtain. Flasch, on the platform, had begun turning handsprings, while Winkler juggled half-a-dozen flaming torches.

As Presto jumped from his arms and perched on a barrel, Sebastian glimpsed the Princess with her tray, ready to make her way through the crowd.

He seized the girl by the shoulders and spun her around. "No, no!" he shouted, while Isabel stared at him, wondering if he had suddenly gone out of his wits. "You can't be seen! The barber! Quick, we must be off!"

Before the girl could reply, Quicksilver hustled up to them.

"What's this, what's this? Out with you, Charles, or those apples will turn moldier than they are! And you," he cried, thrusting fiddle and bow into Sebastian's hands, "to the stage! Adam's already there."

Isabel flung down her tray. At the same time, Madame Sophie, garbed as the Amazon Queen, rode up on the swaybacked horse, and her arrival only added to the confusion.

Quicksilver, without further ado, collared the desperate and struggling Sebastian and propelled him bodily onto the stage.

Adam, perking up at the sight of a fellow player, lumbered forward, paws outstretched. Sebastian, whose only thought was to reach Isabel again, tried to avoid the oncoming bear and escape from the platform. But Adam, mistaking Sebastian's attempts for a game, blocked him at every turn; and the two danced back and forth.

The audience, without the faintest notion of what was actually happening, clapped their hands and egged on the two supposed performers.

"Hurrah for the bear!" shouted one.

"Hurrah for the clown!" cried another.

"See the look on his face!" put in a third. "I've never seen anything so funny. You'd swear the fellow truly means to run off!"

Sebastian redoubled his frantic efforts, but the more he strove to flee the louder the onlookers roared with laughter. Suddenly he heard a burst of applause. Adam halted and turned in his tracks.

Thinking at last to make good his escape, Sebastian was about to dash through the wings. Then he stopped short. Princess Isabel had come onto the stage.

She had changed from boy's garb to the particolored

bodice and short, gold-spangled skirts of a circus dancer.
Over her face she wore a black half mask; and in her
hair, Quicksilver's glass gems sparkled as brilliantly as
real ones. Until now, Sebastian had never seen the Princess in anything but jacket and breeches, and he gaped at
the vision. Taken aback, he blinked in amazement while
Isabel curtseyed most charmingly, and he stood utterly
dumbstruck until Quicksilver's voice brought him back
to his senses.

"Do something! Anything!" Quicksilver hissed, poking
his head around the curtain. "Don't stand there like an
idiot! The fiddle! Play! And smile! Smile!"

Knees quaking, choking as if sand filled his gullet, Sebastian tucked the violin under his chin. At the first
notes, Adam pricked up his ears. His sorrowful eyes
brightened as he cocked his head toward the music.

Isabel took hold of the bear's paw as gracefully as if he
were the most elegant courtier in the Glorietta. The
huge animal changed his shambling gait to follow Sebastian's measures and in another moment, guided by the
Princess, the hulking Adam stepped after her, pirouet-
ting so lightly his heavy hind paws seemed not to touch
the ground.

As for Sebastian, his hands trembled, his knees
knocked, and he shook so violently with fright that he
feared he would be unable to play at all. But no sooner
did he bow the first notes than he lost all thought of the
onlookers, the barber, the Gallimaufry-Theatricus, and
even Princess Isabel.

Now his fingers moved of themselves, each note perfect, each tone true, with a skill he had never known he
possessed. He heard nothing but the music; and though

he was no longer sure whether it came from the instrument, from himself, or from the singing head at the scroll, he wanted only to plunge deeper into the flood of shimmering sound.

Yet the more beautifully the violin played, the more he felt his own strength failing. While his heart urged him to keep on, and the music itself seemed to implore him not to stop, a strange terror filled him, and he dared continue no longer. Fearful, yet grief-stricken, he forced himself to wrench the bow from the strings. When the music ceased, it was like a death.

Only then was he aware of the villagers shouting and cheering at the top of their voices. The curtain dropped. Isabel had vanished from the stage. Quicksilver was pummeling him on the back and yelling in his ear:

"Bravo, my boy! Bravo, bravissimo! You're as fine a fiddler as Lelio himself. Better, indeed! Splendid! Superb! Hurry, Winkler, pass the hat while the rustics are still in generous spirits. If there's enough latecomers, we might have a go at it all over again. Magnificent! We've a new star turn in the Gallimaufry-Theatricus!"

Flasch, standing apart, gave Sebastian a venomous glance, turned on his heel, and strode away. But Madame Sophie flung her arms around Sebastian, and at the same time whispered to him:

"Don't let Quicksilver work you to the bone. Tell him you'll play no more tonight, for you look drawn through a knothole. Be firm with him, or he'll want you to fiddle your fingers off, and swindle you out of your ten toes into the bargain."

All this was the least of Sebastian's concerns as he ran from the stage. The villagers were leaving the field.

There was no sign of the barber. Heaving a sigh of relief, he turned back to look for Isabel. Presto, seeing his master, jumped from the barrel top and mewed insistently as he padded to the array of boxes and hampers. Sebastian followed him.

Isabel, still in her spangled costume, her mask thrown aside, was crouched behind a packing crate. Sebastian hurried to her.

"We're safe!" he cried. "The bloodhound's gone!"

Instead of sharing his jubilation, Isabel burst into tears.

"We have never been so humiliated in our lives!" she sobbed. "To make a spectacle of ourselves on a public stage! We shall never be able to justify such lack of deportment to the Court Metaphysician, the Lord Chamberlain, the First Minister of Protocol—"

"What!" cried Sebastian. "On top of all your troubles you're worried about explaining to a pack of the Regent's courtiers how you saved your life? They'd rather you lost it!"

The Princess only wept harder. Though Sebastian put a consoling hand on her arm, he had no hope of ever stopping such a flood. After some moments, however, the girl's sobs changed to sniffling; Isabel blew her nose as royally as she could in the circumstances, and gave him a sidelong glance. "The implication of your preceding remarks was that we—that our attempts—may we assume that we performed satisfactorily?"

"None better!" Sebastian exclaimed. "You did as well as if you'd been born in the Gallimaufry-Theatricus instead of the Glorietta. As for that costume you made such a fuss about—why, it becomes you better than a pair of breeches."

Isabel blushed. "We presume your statement is meant to be of a complimentary nature. As for ourselves, we must commend you on your own achievement. It was—it has never been our pleasure to hear such music."

"Lelio's fiddle," Sebastian murmured, touching the violin with renewed wonder. "I can't understand the thing. I wasn't playing it, it was—well, it was playing me." He shook his head. "The music was beyond my skill. The voice, the tone—it was not of my doing. I didn't want to stop. It seemed that if I went on, somehow I'd hear music even more beautiful. But at the last moment I was afraid, I turned away from it. Now I'm sorry I did. I fear I might have lost the chance. I must try again."

Isabel did not reply, but looked at the violin fearfully.

Sebastian shook his head. "Quicksilver called it accursed. I didn't believe him then, and I believe him even less now. Accursed? Why, just the contrary! Bring me to grief? How can a fiddle like this bring anything but joy?"

He turned at the sound of footsteps behind him and saw Quicksilver with Madame Sophie.

"So there you are, the two of you," said the impresario. He looked sternly at Sebastian. "Did you talk about moonshine and make-believe? Well, my lad, that servant of yours is made of both. Will you tell me straight out who your lackey is? Or shall I tell you?"

XIX ∽ How Sebastian Played Too Well

ISABEL paled, and Sebastian jumped to his feet.

"Aha, you had me well fooled!" Quicksilver declared, gravely shaking his head. "It took the sharp eye of that perfect flower of womanhood, the ravishing Madame Sophie, to see the truth. Charles? Not a bit of it! Shall I tell you more? Very well. I know both of you for exactly what you are."

Isabel covered her face with her hands. Sebastian flung a protective arm about her shoulders.

"It's plain as my nose," said Quicksilver. Then, seeing Sebastian's alarm, he threw back his head and laughed heartily. "Never fear! I'm not one to sunder a pair of lovebirds!"

Isabel gasped. Sebastian was altogether at a loss for an answer, and before he could blurt out any sort of denial or explanation, Quicksilver nudged him sharply in the ribs and declared:

"Admit it! Admit it, for you can't do otherwise! You've run off. And why? I can tell you that, for nothing's easier to guess. Your families were against the match. And the two of you, head over heels in love! What else to do but run off to be wed!"

Quicksilver twirled his mustache and gave Sebastian a knowing wink. "Sly dog! But I understand it well. That garden of delight, Madame Sophie, and I did the same in our youth. The precious jewel would still be trundling a fish-barrow if I hadn't snatched her away."

"Ah, look at the poor dearie," Madame Sophie put in, beaming at Isabel. "So shy and flustered she can't get a word out. But all the world loves a lover, and your secret's safe with us. When you set the wedding day, I'll lend you my own bridal veil—if Quicksilver hasn't scissored it up for costumes. Come now, you shall sleep in the van. A bride-to-be should have all her comforts, for she may have few enough of them after she's wed."

As Madame Sophie led the still speechless Isabel to the wagon, Quicksilver turned to Sebastian.

"You'll stay with us in the Gallimaufry-Theatricus, my boy. Indeed, I'd not let either of you go. You'll have a brilliant career, both of you. Take the example of Madame Sophie and myself. You'll be famous, my lad, that I promise. How does that strike you?"

Seeing Sebastian still openmouthed, Quicksilver nodded. "I understand, my boy. You can't believe your good fortune. Small wonder you're struck dumb. Beyond your wildest dreams, eh? Of course it is. Too much to grasp all at once: heading the bill of the Gallimaufry-Theatricus! And more yet! But I'll save it, I don't want to overload you with so much honor so quickly. But tomorrow, my boy—ah, tomorrow I promise you a splendid surprise!"

As the impresario turned and followed the Thornless

Rose, Sebastian collapsed onto a hamper and clapped his hands to his head. "Ah, Presto, Presto, where does the world begin and the Gallimaufry-Theatricus leave off? The Princess—from lackey to dancing girl to blushing bride-to-be! And Quicksilver, who's hoaxed so many others, has finally hoaxed himself! He takes us for a pair of lovers, and I think he'll see us that way no matter what I tell him! Whatever gave him the notion, I can't imagine. Unless he's been in the Theatricus so long that he can't tell truth from moonshine. Or, indeed, is all of it moonshine?"

He picked up the violin. "All? All but this. I'm sure it's the only true thing in the Gallimaufry-Theatricus. And poor Quicksilver thinks the fiddle's accursed!"

Even as he held it in his hand, the instrument murmured and its music seemed impatient to be freed. The melody he had played haunted his memory and he longed to hear it again. And so he would have done, but he was suddenly weary to the marrow of his bones, half ill, and for a moment feared he would topple to the ground.

He barely found strength to change from the clown's costume to his own garments. He sank down amid the boxes and hampers, with Presto curled in the crook of his arm. Even then, he felt uneasy and restless. Despite his exhaustion, it was some while before he slept.

When Sebastian awoke at daybreak, his first thought was of the fiddle. He climbed hastily to his feet. Adam snored under the platform. Quicksilver's van was dark, and the troupe gave no sign of rousing. While Presto unhurriedly stretched, yawned, and began his morning washing, Sebastian went to the far side of the field.

There he settled himself on a stump and eagerly put the violin under his chin. As before, he had no sooner drawn the bow across the strings than the voice of the instrument swelled about him, lovelier than he remembered it. Again he lost himself in the maze of melodies, each fresher, more beautiful, each leading to another like door after door flung open to him. Again he sensed greater music still beyond his reach. But this time he felt a darker current, rising from icy depths, chilling his blood. The melody now seemed to flow from the carved face on the scroll, in a voice that both lured him to keep on and warned him to stop. His heart pounded frightfully. The warning tone sharpened. But the music promised even more superb melodies and Sebastian choked back his fear, determined he would hear them.

He cried out in sudden pain. The voice of the violin fell abruptly silent. Bewildered, he blinked at finding himself once more on the stump. It was full daylight. Presto crouched at his feet.

As Sebastian, still dazed, bent to give him a reassuring pat, he stopped in surprise. On his knee were the marks of Presto's claws, sunk deeply enough to draw blood.

"Why, Your Catliness," Sebastian told him in mock severity, "if my music's not to your liking, you could have found a gentler way of telling me to leave off."

Then he saw Isabel. Instead of the dancer's costume, she wore a gracefully cut gown. Her dark hair, softly combed, fell loose about her shoulders.

Startled a moment, for he had never seen the girl so attired, he jumped to his feet and called out: "Well, you're a handsomer girl than you were a boy. If no one knew better, they might say you look almost like a princess!"

"Our external appearance has been modified at the instigation of Madame Sophie," Isabel replied. "Quicksilver requests your presence, and suggests you wear these," she added, handing a bundle of garments to Sebastian. "We called to you, but our attempts to gain your attention were apparently inaudible."

"I was listening too closely to Lelio's fiddle and heard nothing else," Sebastian replied lightly, unwilling to tell Isabel of the instrument's strange effect. "If Presto hadn't sharpened his claws on me, I might be playing yet."

"We may permit ourselves to state that we listened with pleasure," said Isabel, "and we pray you to continue."

"A royal command to play?" Sebastian cried, "I'll not refuse that!"

Exhausted though he was, he struck up a gay and high-spirited tune; but he had scarcely begun when he broke off, more than ever amazed: not at the instrument but at Isabel.

The usually solemn Princess was laughing wholeheartedly, as delighted as a child.

When the music stopped, Isabel tried with much difficulty to regain her sober expression.

"Our unseemly levity—" she stammered, "—as discomfiting to ourselves as it would be to our Lord Chamberlain. Yet we found ourselves, for reasons incomprehensible, unable to refrain from unintentional hilarity. We assure you it indicates our approval, not our criticism."

"Why, how now!" exclaimed Sebastian, as surprised as the Princess. "It must be a charmed fiddle indeed, if it can make you smile, let alone laugh. I've seen you do neither until this very moment. Very well, let's see if it happens again."

Before he could strike up another tune, Sebastian felt his head start spinning, and his strength flickering away. Shaking with a chill, he fell back against the stump.

Isabel gasped in alarm, and knelt beside him. The giddiness had gone as quickly as it had come. In a few moments, the chill lifted. Embarrassed at his sudden turn, he grinned sheepishly at the Princess, and said:

"I think Lelio's fiddle is a hard taskmaster. I've never played so well nor so easily; yet after I've done, it makes me feel I've never toiled harder in my life."

Isabel looked at the violin uneasily. "If you experience debilitating or deleterious consequences, we urge you, for your own benefit and our mental tranquility, to discontinue such efforts."

"What, give up this fiddle?" Sebastian returned. "I'd sooner part with my skin and bones! The thing has music in it a man would trade his life to hear even once!"

"We should consider that an unfortunate exchange, as unwise as it is distressing, and will not bring ourselves to countenance it."

"Princess, if you could hear its voice as I do—" Sebastian began. He had no chance to say more, for Quicksilver was calling urgently to them. With Isabel and Presto, he made his way as quickly as he could to the stage.

"If you had even guessed a part of the glorious news I have for you," declared the impresario, "you'd not have been tardy to hear it. Did I not promise you a surprise? You shall have it."

Quicksilver raised his arms and struck a pose, looking ready to address an audience of thousands.

"With the engagement of the finest fiddler in Hamelin-Loring," the impresario grandly proclaimed, "the world-famous Gallimaufry-Theatricus proudly consents to bring this remarkable and unique attraction before a public of the most discerning taste and appreciation. As soon as the magnificent Flasch comes back from town with the necessary provisions, as soon as the admirable Winkler hauls down the balloon, and as soon as the delightful Thornless Rose completes her ablutions, we'll set about reaping the rewards in the only place worthy of your performance. In short, my boy—we're going to Loringhold."

xx ∾ How Sebastian Reached for the Moon

No!" cried Isabel. "We shall not—"

"What, what?" exclaimed Quicksilver. "Not go to Loringhold? We'll make as many ducats there as we did pennies last night. There's more waiting for us in the capital than all the northern bumpkins will see in a lifetime. And that's not all my plan. Once the word spreads, as it's sure to do—aha, dare you guess? Of course! A command performance at nothing less than the Glorietta Palace!

"I understand," Quicksilver went on, seeing the horrified look on the faces of Sebastian and Isabel. "You fear the town audiences. Well, you needn't, for they're won as easily as rustics. So never fret, but pack your things and we'll all soon have our fortunes made."

At this, excited by his new prospects, Quicksilver hurried off the stage, calling for Madame Sophie to make ready without delay.

"Loringhold!" Sebastian gasped. "Last place in the world! The Glorietta? Sooner the gallows! Baron Purn-Hessel always took me to task for not playing my best—but now I've played too well!"

He began hastily packing the green bag. "We've got to get out of here and no time to lose—"

Isabel gave a cry of alarm. Sebastian turned and saw Flasch striding across the field. Beside him, red-faced and sweating, their cocked hats on the back of their heads, tramped a pair of town constables.

Sebastian's only thought was to seize Isabel and run for dear life, but one of the constables pulled a pistol from his belt and pointed the muzzle straight at him.

"Stand fast, there," ordered the constable, never lowering the weapon as he glanced quickly at Flasch. "Is that the fellow?"

"It is," replied Flasch, "and have a care with him, for who knows what murderous tricks he has up his sleeve."

"What mad tale are you telling?" Sebastian burst out. "What have you done to us?"

"Only my duty," answered the tumbler. "There's word about in Great Brunswick that a band of cutthroats and brigands laid Darmstel to waste, burning and looting, and leaving a dozen honest folk murdered in their beds. And it was near Darmstel you wormed your way into our company. Where the rest of your villainous crew may be —you know that better than I."

"That's a lie!" cried Sebastian. "No such thing happened in Darmstel. I was there myself!"

"Aha, so you admit it, then," put in the constable. "I'm not surprised. I saw you had a rogue's face the minute I laid eyes on you."

"A real gallows bird," his comrade agreed. "All right, up with your hands, out with your wrists."

Flasch had meanwhile turned to Isabel and, giving her a honeyed glance, said:

"You'll thank me for saving you from such a villain. But I did it gladly. I'd not see such a tender thing as you go astray with the likes of him. No, you'll do better sharing the star turn with me and not some ruffian of a fiddler."

"Serpent!" shouted Quicksilver, shaking his fist at the tumbler. "Whatever's amiss in the Gallimaufry-Theatricus, we don't have the law nosing into it. You've cost us all our fortune, you scoundrel! Begone, I'll have no more of you in the company!"

"Will you not?" replied the tumbler. "What else can you show, then, but a mangy bear and a heavy-footed harridan?"

Hearing this, Madame Sophie shrieked indignantly. The constable brandished his pistol.

"Hold your tongues, all of you," he ordered, "or there'll be more than a fiddler lodged in prison."

"There shall be none lodged in prison," Isabel declared. "Stand away."

The constable blinked at her. "Now there's a vixen! To order us like a captain of dragoons!"

"Have a care, you little minx," his comrade put in, "or that sharp tongue of yours will lead you to sharper trouble."

"Do as we bid you," Isabel replied. "Set him free and be gone." The girl drew herself up to her full height. "This is our royal command. We are Isabel Charlotte Theodora Fredericka, Princess of Hamelin-Loring."

Sebastian cried out for Isabel to keep silent. Quicksilver, his mustache trembling in astonishment, stared at the girl. Madame Sophie, as much taken aback as the rest of the company, burst out:

"I knew it! I guessed from the first she was a fine lady. Indeed, the Princess Isabel herself. She could be no less!"

So saying, the Thornless Rose dipped a splendid curtsey. But the constable threw back his head and laughed.

"I've heard many a tale, but none to match this!"

His comrade, who had been watching Isabel closely, elbowed him sharply in the ribs and whispered:

"Suppose she's what she claims?"

"Eh? Eh? Suppose she's the Princess?" replied the constable. "And suppose you're a fool! She's no more princess than I am!" His laughter, however, died abruptly, his red face creased in a frown, and his eyes darted back and forth. "No chance of it," he muttered. "Then again—"

"Pay her no heed," Sebastian desperately cried. "She's no princess, but a circus dancer! A giddy girl who fancies herself better than what she is!"

"Hold your tongue," snapped the constable. "Since you're the accused, nothing you say can be taken into any account whatever, as you're surely lying in the first place."

"He'd lie to save his own skin," said the other officer, "but the wench is trying to save it for him. So if he's lying, then how do we know she's not indeed telling the truth?"

"Ah, that's deep thinking," replied the constable. "You've a clever head on your shoulders." He nodded several times, looking as if he were cracking walnuts between his teeth. "There's nothing for it," he said at last, "but to have all of them to the magistrate. As for you," he added, turning to Isabel, "if you're the Princess you'll not say you weren't treated with courtesy. If you're a circus dancer, take my word it will go hard as nails with you. Now, quick march!"

Sebastian, seeing no other course, reluctantly picked up his bag and fiddle. Presto hopped onto his shoulder.

"Here, what's this?" demanded the constable, swinging his pistol toward the cat.

"He's mine and he'll go where I go," Sebastian declared.

"That he will," the constable said gruffly. "We'll have him up as evidence, too."

With one officer in front and the other bringing up the rear, Isabel, Sebastian, and the cast of the Gallimaufry-Theatricus made their way across the field. As they did, Sebastian's heart quickened at the sight of the red-and-yellow sphere bobbing gently at the end of its tether. But the constables had not put away their pistols and he saw no chance of reaching the balloon.

That moment, Adam, still napping under the stage, roused and uncurled himself. Seeing Sebastian and the fiddle, the bear grunted happily and rose on his hind legs, eager for a dance.

The startled constable roared in terror, brought up his pistol, but fired so hastily that the ball went whistling harmlessly through the air.

Adam, lumbering on, seized the fellow in his burly arms and swung him about, while the officer howled and bawled and fought vainly to free himself.

The second constable, now at a loss whether to defend his comrade from the monstrous bear or to guard the prisoners, brandished his pistol wildly and brought it to aim at the first target of opportunity: Sebastian's head.

Presto gave an earsplitting yowl, leaped from Sebastian's shoulder to the constable's outstretched arm, and clung there with all his sharp claws. The man shouted an oath as he stumbled off balance and the pistol went spinning out of his hands. Seizing Isabel's arm, Sebastian raced for the balloon.

"Halt! Halt!" bellowed the constable. Leaving his comrade still in Adam's furry embrace, he whipped out a saber and made off after the fleeing pair; though before he could go a pace, Presto darted through his legs, tripped him up, and sent him sprawling to the ground.

Madame Sophie, meantime, had snatched up a pole from the stage; no sooner did the constable regain his feet than he tumbled down again under her vigorous blows. Quicksilver seized the fellow's saber and waved it in the air, threatening to carve Flasch into mutton.

Reaching the swaying basket, Sebastian tossed in his bag and fiddle, hoisted Isabel over the side, and struggled to untie the mooring line.

"Presto!" he called, glancing back but seeing nothing of the white cat.

The constable, free at last of Adam's grip, was running heavily across the field. Sebastian glimpsed a white streak bolting faster than a rabbit through the grass. In another instant, with the officer no more than half-a-dozen strides behind, Presto gained the balloon and leaped aboard.

The rope, now unloosened, whipped out of Sebastian's hands. Isabel screamed. Sebastian saw her terror-stricken face as the balloon shot upward.

XXI ∽ How the Travelers Came to Earth

He clutched vainly at the basket as it soared above his head. The dangling rope went lashing by. He seized it and was borne aloft with a bone-rattling jolt, heels kicking in the air, while the great red-and-yellow bubble sped faster toward the open sky.

Swinging like a pendulum, Sebastian clung for dear life to the rope's end. In a downward glance, he saw the two constables shaking their fists at him. Adam raised his shaggy arms in a sad farewell. The figures of Quicksilver, Madame Sophie, Flasch, and Winkler, and the wagons of the Gallimaufry-Theatricus dwindled to the size of dolls and toys.

Hands turning numb, and in his last strength, Sebastian hauled himself upward and with a final heave tumbled into the basket, where he fell in a gasping heap onto the wicker flooring. Isabel flung her arms about him and Presto scrambled to his side.

Sebastian crawled to his feet while the sphere, halting its upward climb, steadied itself in the air. Now that Quicksilver's balloon had borne the fugitives beyond the constables' reach, Sebastian cast about for a way back to earth. Bags of sand hung at the rim of the basket. However, he saw that emptying these would only lighten the load and send it higher.

"Princess, forgive me," Sebastian groaned. "You saved my life, but I've put yours in worse danger."

Though Isabel's eyes were wide with fright, she managed to regain some of her composure as she answered:

"Our concern, as we have previously stated, is not for our personal safety. We have, instead, realized that our presence occasions only misfortune for others. We have no desire to impose further tribulations on our subjects, collectively or—or individually. Should we be extricated from this unpremeditated situation, we must seriously question the plausibility of continuing in our enterprise."

"What, do you mean to cry quits now?" Sebastian exclaimed. "Concerned for your subjects? Will they be better off with Grinssorg on the throne? And you, his bride? How long before you'd have a carriage accident, as your parents did? Or just happen to tumble out a window? Why, you're safer even in Quicksilver's balloon than in the Glorietta!"

But the balloon dropped suddenly downward and set Sebastian back on his heels. Presto, curiously investigating the basket, had pounced on a dangling cord and was hanging onto it like a sailor climbing a ship's rigging.

"Have a care—get away from that," Sebastian called. Then he realized the cord was affixed to a valve at the bottom of the sphere. By tugging on it, the cat had released some of the buoyant air.

"Presto! You've shown me how to bring us down!"

Sebastian was about to haul on the rope when he

stopped short. The balloon was drifting at a good rate toward a line of distant peaks.

"Our luck's not done!" he exclaimed. "It's just begun. We're better off in the air than on the ground. Look there! We're heading north. Before you know it, we'll be in Upper Cassel!"

And, in fact, the brightly painted sphere was bearing the fugitives surely and steadily in the direction of Prince Frederick's realm and to safety.

All day the balloon held its northward course. The fields and hills flattened into patches of green and yellow, stitched with glittering threads of streams. The air, clear and cool, hummed gently through the rigging. Isabel silently watched the oncoming mountains. Presto settled comfortably on a coil of rope. And Sebastian, growing used to such a peculiar means of travel, began to feel more lighthearted than he had since the Baron turned him out.

"I understand now why Quicksilver drew crowds to his balloon," he said. "It's the best way I know to leave your cares behind you. When I think of all that's happened to us on the ground, I'd be happy to stay in the clouds."

Isabel bit her lip and murmured, more to herself than to Sebastian:

"We are not disinclined to reiterate your observation."

"Well, never fear, Princess," replied Sebastian. "You'll soon be safe with your uncle. Now that I see how to deal with these ropes and sandbags, I'm sure I can set us down in the middle of Prince Frederick's own palace!"

Isabel glanced at him. "And you—what are your intentions concerning your future itinerary?"

"If you mean *where* shall I go," Sebastian answered, "I've no idea. In Darmstel, I wanted to join the Captain, and I still do. But how I'll ever find him now, I can't imagine."

"Will you—will you not give further consideration to accepting a situation at our court? We trust that your incomprehensible desire to associate yourself with such a dangerous brigand as the Captain will not replace your musical endeavors."

Sebastian shook his head. "Give up music? No—it's strange, but I'm fonder of it than I ever thought I could be."

"We admire your playing," said Isabel, "but it would seem to us that you, in addition, have become aware of certain aspects of music that we, unfortunately, have not been entirely able to share."

"Why, Princess," replied Sebastian, "you make it sound as if I'd gone off where no one else could follow. And yet, indeed sometimes it feels that way. Did Lelio go on the same journey? I wish I could have met him and talked with him. It might have cheered us both."

"May we venture to inquire whether such unique melodies and harmonies could not be committed to paper, both for their permanent preservation and the edification of other performers and listeners?"

"Write them down? I don't know—I'd never thought of it. That's work for a composer, not a fiddler, and beyond my skill. I'm surprised that Lelio's fiddle plays for me in the first place. Quicksilver told me it would answer only to a master worthy of it."

"Accepting the veracity of his statement," said Isabel, "then we must conclude you have undervalued your abilities. In whatever degree of development they may be at the moment, you should recognize unmistakable potentialities."

"Are you saying I have the makings of a true musician? Baron Purn-Hessel's Fourth Fiddle? That would be the best joke of all! No, Princess, I'll be glad if I have the makings of a true balloonist and bring you safely to your uncle's court."

"We recognize, commend, and express gratitude for your sense of duty to the Royal House—" Isabel began.

"Royal House?" replied Sebastian. "You talk as though you were a door and a window and a flight of steps! No, Princess, if I have any duty it's to no Royal House, but the girl who crowned me with a bucket in the Golden Stag."

He suddenly became aware that he had taken Isabel's hand. The Princess lowered her eyes, but made no attempt to withdraw. Sebastian hesitated as his words dried up in his throat. At that moment, the balloon swung about sharply and the basket spun like a top.

Isabel clung to him as the rigging screamed. Sebastian realized with dismay the wind had shifted. With the mountains just before them, and the safe haven of Upper Cassel nearly in sight, the basket was flung into an invisible tide that bore it along at top speed in the opposite direction. He braced himself in a corner and tried with all his might to keep the Princess from being tossed out of the madly pitching wicker shell. Presto, ears flat against his head, dug his claws into the flooring.

Hoping to gain height and escape the clutch of the gale, Sebastian tore open the sandbags; to no avail, for the balloon sped faster.

The sun had dropped like a stone, and the balloon plunged blindly through a starless night, swallowed in a black flood that drowned the fugitives in darkness. To worsen matters, a lashing rain set in, drenching them to the skin while trees of lightning crackled across the sky.

"Bring us down!" Isabel pleaded. "We'll go no farther!"

"Hold fast!" Sebastian shouted. "Better the storm than Grinssorg's bloodhounds. The wind must stop!"

But the storm did not slacken. All night the balloon raced on its own path. Only at dawn did the wind at last die away. By then, they had been so pitched and tossed that Sebastian, stumbling to the side of the basket, had not the least idea where it had borne them.

He could make out nothing through the blue haze of mist, and only judged the balloon was losing height, dropping steadily each moment, and gaining speed the while. It swung wildly and tumbled him against the side of the basket.

Down they plummeted. As the clouds broke away, he glimpsed rooftops spinning below. A crosswind sent the balloon scudding along a row of chimney pots, snapping them off like pipestems, and the jolt nearly sent the voyagers flying out in a shower of bricks and mortar. The basket tilted, dropped sharply, and, with a ripping and cracking of broken wicker, came to a sudden halt.

Sebastian, skidding from the basket, saw the red-and-yellow bag slowly collapsing into what seemed a lake. The rigging had caught and tangled on a great swan of bronze.

Seeing Isabel and Presto unharmed, he gave a glad cry:

"Safe at last, all of us with a whole skin! And a royal welcome from Prince Frederick!"

Isabel's face showed no relief, only terror. "The Swan Fountain!" she gasped. "Upper Cassel? No! It's Loringhold!"

HALF dragging Isabel behind him, with Presto clinging to his shoulder, Sebastian splashed through the water and leaped the stone wall. The crashing balloon had
brought idlers and passersby from all corners of the
square. Windows were flung open, heads popped out,
onlookers shouted and pointed at the gaudy bubble
collapsing slowly into the fountain, and all were so
caught up by the sight they paid no mind whatever to
the fleeing occupants.

In despair at coming to earth in the middle of Loringhold, hedged and hemmed by the growing crowd, Sebastian could only struggle blindly through the mob, his
one thought to take Isabel from the scene as far and as
fast as he could.

The commotion had brought a troop of the Regent's
dragoons galloping into the square. Their furious faces
were scarlet as their tunics; and, having no idea what
caused the uproar, they pulled out their sabers and
flailed at everything in their way. Sebastian barely escaped having his head lopped off his shoulders as he

snatched Isabel from the horsemen's path and stumbled into an alley.

They ran to the end of the passageway. The stream of townsfolk fleeing the dragoons forced them on until he and Isabel were thrust into a wider but more crowded thoroughfare.

Here Sebastian found himself in the midst of a throng of hawkers and hucksters trundling barrows of vegetables and crying their wares at the top of their voices; hatters with hats piled in towers on their heads; piemen; pin sellers; beggars bawling for charity.

Spying a break in the crowd, Sebastian plunged across the street. His moment was ill chosen, for he nearly tumbled under the wheels of a cart. Isabel screamed. The horses reared, and the cursing driver tried to turn them, only to collide with a handsomely lacquered and gilded sedan chair, whose four bearers struggled to keep their burden upright.

The sedan chair tottered as the footmen lost their grip on the carrying shafts, and tilted so sharply that the door sprang open, to send the chair's occupant bursting out and tumbling in a heap on the cobbles. Presto jumped on top of the vehicle while Sebastian bent to help the outraged occupant to his feet.

The man's cocked hat, edged in gold braid, had fallen into a puddle; mud befouled the knees of his breeches, and his wig was tipped askew. Sebastian's jaw dropped, for there was no mistaking the heavy-jowled, toadlike face of The Purse.

But The Purse showed no sign of recognizing Sebastian. Wattles trembling with rage, Count Lobelieze gave him no more heed than a cobblestone. Puffing indignantly as Sebastian hauled him upright, he snatched a gold-headed cane and set about belaboring the footmen.

Next instant, however, The Purse caught sight of Isabel.

Though she turned hastily away, the courtier knew her immediately. The cane he was about to bring down on the skull of a cowering lackey stayed frozen in midair. The Purse's eyes bulged, ready to pop from his head, and his jowls blew in and out as he stammered:

"Puh . . . puh . . . Princess?"

Isabel spun around and plunged into the crowd of gawking onlookers, who fell back, too astonished to do more than let her pass. Presto leaped from the top of the sedan chair and darted ahead. Sebastian took to his heels after them, leaving the bewildered Purse with cane still upraised.

Presto streaked around a corner, darted down a twisting street, turned sharply without losing speed, then spurted ahead so quickly that it was all the two fugitives could do to keep the tip of his tail in sight.

Along the crooked alley, where the upper windows of crumbling buildings jutted within arm's length of each other, Sebastian and Isabel picked their way through mire and rubble.

"What place is this?" Isabel gasped, as much from the variety of odors assailing her nose as from her exertions. "Where are you taking us?"

"Ask Presto," Sebastian returned, "for I think he knows Loringhold better than we do."

The white cat by then had bounded into a dank maze

of archways and sunless courtyards where goats bleated at the ends of their tethers and chickens pecked among midden heaps. Presto shot inside the first open door, past a gaunt, heavy-boned woman bent over a steaming tub of laundry which she stirred with a wooden pole.

The washerwoman started at the sudden arrival of the cat, who jumped onto her ironing board; then, seeing Sebastian and Isabel in the doorway, she flung up the pole and held it like a cudgel, as if these breathless strangers were about to rob her, murder her, or make off with her baskets of laundry.

"You're none of my customers," she cried. "Tell your business and be off with you!"

"My cat—" Sebastian began, by way of the first explanation that came to him. "He ran away—we were following him."

"Your cat?" the washerwoman retorted. "Yours? That's one lie to begin with. I've seen that white fur and blue eyes before. And the size of him! No mistake! I've given him food more than once, though he'd never stay with me. A wild stray that no one claimed; and he took no one for his master. He was king of the rooftops and alleys until he went his way again. Who knows what he's been up to since then?" She looked sharply at Sebastian and the Princess. "And you? What have you been up to? I know trouble so well I can smell it in the air, and both of you reek of it. What are you? Sneak thieves? Cutpurses?"

"We've done no crime," Sebastian hurriedly assured the washerwoman. "I'm no cutpurse, but a fiddler. And this gentlewoman—"

"Gentlewoman!" burst out the washerwoman. "Next,

you'll be telling me she's the Princess of Hamelin-Loring! A good thing she's not, for I'd give her a piece of my mind and all of my stick! Princess! I'd Princess her so well she'd not forget it. My husband in prison because he grumbled at the tax on bread! My brother run off two jumps ahead of the hangman to join the Captain! Ah, ah, tell me nothing of the nobility, for I want no part of them. No more do I want any share of whatever stew you've tumbled into. Out, out! Be off with you!"

"Give us at least a moment's rest," Sebastian pleaded, seeing that Isabel had gone quite pale and had sunk down on a wooden bench.

The washerwoman eyed him suspiciously, and finally nodded curtly. "Well enough, but no more than that. You're on the shady side of the law, that's for sure."

Sebastian heaved a sigh of relief, for the respite would at least give him time to collect his wits. But a moment later he was choking with dismay. Isabel had risen to her feet and was looking squarely at the washerwoman.

"In view of your expressed opinions concerning the Royal House, we do not consider it appropriate to accept your assistance under false pretenses. Although we are far from content at your estimation of ourselves as miscreants, the peril of our situation obliges us to apprise you of the peril to yourself. We are indeed Princess Isabel Charlotte Theodora—"

"What?" shouted the washerwoman, her face turning as gray as her own wash water. The Princess had spoken in a tone that left no room for disbelief, and for a moment Sebastian feared the woman would carry out her threat and start flailing away with her stick.

Instead, the washerwoman sat down heavily in a basket of laundry, clapped her hands to her head, and began moaning loudly.

"The ruin of me! The Princess! In my laundry! What trouble will this bring? Out, out, and let me be! I've never seen either of you! Nor your cat! Be off!"

XXIII ❧ How the Princess Mended Her Speech

SEBASTIAN, in despair that Isabel had given herself away, saw nothing but to tell as quickly as he could how they had fallen into their plight. When he finished, the washerwoman only looked more distressed, and shook her stick at the Princess, declaring:

"No thanks to you for putting me in such a pickle! There's no love lost between the Royal House and me. But I'll take anyone's part against the Regent—even yours! If you were a straightforward, honest pair of thieves, I could help you better. But this matter's too deep for me."

The washerwoman pondered for a time, then reluctantly climbed to her feet.

"So be it," she sighed. "I never thought I'd see the day when royalty needed my help—nor the day I'd give it. Stay here. Keep out of sight. I'll do what needs doing, if there's any hope for you to be gone from Loringhold."

Still shaking her head and muttering to herself, the washerwoman hurried from the laundry.

"Ah, Princess," cried Sebastian, "why did you tell her who you were? The Purse knows you're in Loringhold and as soon as that barrel of lard gets to the palace, Grinssorg will know it, too. Better to pass as thieves and cutpurses, as the washerwoman thought us."

"We find it unseemly and distasteful to conceal our identity when the issue involves the safety of one of our subjects," replied Isabel, looking as downcast as if the washerwoman had given her a sound drubbing with the stick instead of with her tongue. "Once on our throne again, we shall thoroughly investigate her grievances. But we are puzzled at the degree of animosity, even hostility, demonstrated by this good woman toward ourselves. Our First Minister always assured us that we enjoyed the affection of our subjects. Is it possible we placed ingenuous, though unmerited, confidence in his assurances? Or, incredible as it may be, that our First Minister—"

"That he stuffed your head with nonsense?" put in Sebastian. "Like all your Court Metaphysicians, Royal What-Have-Yous, and Imperial Donkeys! He does the Regent's bidding, says the Regent's words—lucky that you had spirit enough to run off when you did. You'd not only have been Grinssorg's bride; if he didn't kill you, he'd addle your brains and turn you into a puppet!"

Instead of being scandalized at Sebastian's reference to imperial donkeys, the Princess looked at him thoughtfully a long moment. "We have always been instructed that a monarch must heed the advice of learned councillors. If what you say is true, they have misled us. But if what they say is true—you have misled us. Alas, alas, since our flight from the palace we've been able to make little sense of anything, and have found nothing to be at all as we supposed."

"Nor have I," Sebastian replied, smiling ruefully. "Between the Merry Host, Quicksilver's Theatricus, murderers disguised as barbers. . . . To find the truth of the matter? Indeed, I think my fiddle's the only place I'll find it."

"Then you are fortunate," Isabel said wistfully. "You have found music. But what shall we find? How shall we even begin to search?"

Sebastian shook his head. "To find what you value most? I think that must be a different matter for each of us. Quicksilver has his Theatricus, and I my fiddle. But what a Princess may find—you must answer that for yourself."

"Our subjects are of primary concern to us," Isabel replied. "Yes, on the most careful reflection, we may say their well-being counts for us to the same degree that your fiddle counts for you. And yet, despite our intentions, we experience difficulty in conveying our attitude and our subjects have equal difficulty in comprehending it."

"Why, Princess, I think it's only because they don't know you," Sebastian said. "I don't mean as Princess of Hamelin-Loring, but as yourself, no more no less. So, be yourself and the rest should come easily."

"Be ourselves? We should be happy to achieve that condition. Unfortunately, we have never been instructed in such a pursuit."

"You can be sure you haven't," Sebastian said. "That would be the last thing in the world the Regent wants. But if you'll listen to a fiddler who knows nothing about such weighty matters, you can start easily. Next time you talk with your subjects, you might mend your speech, to begin with. It may serve at court, but nowhere else. So

—speak straight out! Say what's in your heart to say, as simply as you can, and have done!"

The girl brightened. "If this is your suggestion, we shall endeavor—" She hesitated an instant. "That is, we shall try."

"Bravo!" cried Sebastian. "The Regent's councillors tried to turn you into a puppet. With practice, you'll soon turn yourself back into a girl!"

Thanks to her drenching in the Swan Fountain, Isabel had begun to shiver. At Sebastian's urging, she withdrew to a storeroom at the back of the laundry, there to change into the boy's attire Nicholas had refurbished for her.

The garments Quicksilver had given Sebastian were not only drier than his own but, as he now saw, considerably handsomer. The jacket and waistcoat, though tattered and threadbare in the lining, were, on the outside, splendidly brocaded. This, he judged, was the costume Quicksilver had meant him to wear for the triumphant arrival of the Gallimaufry-Theatricus in Loringhold.

"But I fear it will be a long day before I play Lelio's fiddle in Loringhold," he told himself, "or anywhere else, for the matter of that."

Nevertheless, he was glad for the fresh clothing and by no means displeased at its effect.

"Quicksilver was right," he said to himself. "Appearance is what counts. In these, at least I'll not be taken for a sneak thief. As for you," he added to Presto, nesting comfortably in a heap of soiled laundry, "you're lucky no one takes you for anything but a cat. And yet—those louts in Dorn thought you a witch! So that may be the way of the world with cats and fiddlers alike."

Some while had passed without any sign of the washer-woman, and Sebastian had grown more and more uneasy, pacing back and forth, at every moment pressing his eye to the shutters and peering into the courtyard.

"What's she up to?" he muttered. "She couldn't have meant to turn us over to the constables, or they'd be here long before now."

He squinted through the shutter again. The yard was empty except for a few scrawny chickens. A beggar had come shambling from an alleyway: a huge fellow, with a black beard sprawled across his face. A sack hung from his shoulder, his hat had more holes in it than a sieve; the patches on his grimy cloak were as tattered as the garment itself, and they flapped like crows' wings as he lurched along on a heavy crutch.

Sebastian, about to turn away, shouted an alarm. The beggar, glancing around him, had taken the crutch from under his arm and was striding as quickly as any man on two legs toward the laundry.

XXIV ⤷ How Sebastian Escaped from a Beggar

BLOODHOUND!" Sebastian cried. "Fooled once by a false barber! Not again by a false beggar!"

Cursing the washerwoman's treachery, and himself for trusting her, he tossed the violin into the bag, seized Presto, thrust him in along with it, and cast about for an escape. The storeroom had neither door nor window, and the only way out of the laundry led through the courtyard.

Presto, choosing this of all moments to turn stubborn, began struggling free of the bag until it was all Sebastian could do to keep the cat from jumping out. Warning Isabel that their safest course lay in running for their lives, he unbolted the door and flung it open—only to come face to face with his pursuer.

"So there's the two of you," declared the beggar. "Quick now, come along as I tell you—"

Shouting for Isabel to flee, Sebastian threw himself against the man, who brought up his crutch to fend off this unexpected attack. Next instant, Sebastian saw his opponent stumble backward, roaring furiously.

The Princess had overturned a wash tub, drenching

the beggar in a flood of scalding, soapy water. Snatching up the washerwoman's pole, she cudgeled him as soundly as the washerwoman had threatened to cudgel her.

Isabel's attack sent the astonished fellow slipping, sliding, and tumbling head over heels. Stunned, the beggar floundered in the suds. Seizing the instant for escape, Sebastian rushed the girl from the laundry, out the courtyard, and into the alleyways, dodging and turning until they were sure the bloodhound was far behind.

"Well, Princess, you've a stouter arm than I guessed," he told Isabel when at last they dared slacken their pace. "And lucky I saw that villain for what he was! But Loringhold's a trap. Somehow we've got to be clear of it."

However, it soon dawned on him that he had no notion which, of all the streets and byways, could lead to the town gate with least risk; or even in which direction such an escape lay. And Isabel, seldom allowed beyond the palace grounds, admitted being as lost in her own capital as Sebastian himself.

"We'll remedy that," Sebastian declared, for he had sighted a band of urchins chasing each other back and forth across the alleyway like a dozen kittens, and he saw no danger in questioning them. He called out to the tallest of the ragamuffins, but the boy and his playmates were too caught up in their game to pay him any heed.

"I'll not be Regent any more," cried one. "Turn about, now! Have a care, I'm the Captain!"

"That you're not!" retorted the taller boy, shaking a wooden slat under his comrade's nose. "It's my sword, so I'll be what I choose!"

"I'll be the Captain!" piped up a towheaded little girl

in a grimy apron, and reached to pull the slat from the ragamuffin's hand. "Or else I'll be Regent and kill all of you!"

"You'll be neither," the boy returned. "You're a stupid girl, so you'll be Princess or nothing at all."

"I'll not! You can't make me!" The girl set to bawling and sniveling. "I'll not be Princess! Nobody wants to be her!"

Isabel, overhearing this exchange, looked unhappier than the child, and went to her, saying:

"As pretty as you are, and not want to be a Princess and live in a palace?"

"Of course I do," the girl answered. "But I don't want to be Princess Isabel, that silly thing! And a mean, ugly, wretched creature, besides!"

"Wretched, that's true," replied Isabel. "But mean and ugly? Have you ever seen her?"

"No," said the little girl, "but I'm sure she is."

"Enough, enough," Sebastian put in. "Tell us how to find the town gate, and how a fellow might go if he wanted no one to see him."

The tall boy deigned at last to notice Sebastian and said, in a very matter-of-fact manner, as if it were the most ordinary thing in the world:

"What, are the constables after you?"

The other children had come to crowd around the fugitives. Seeing Presto pop his head out of the bag, they began yelling at the top of their voices:

"A cat with blue eyes!"

"What more's in the sack?"

"Is that a real fiddle?"

"Give us a tune!"

"Give us a penny!"

Sebastian took all this in good part, although the urchins had set about hanging onto his coattails and tugging at the bag.

"Little ones, little ones, time presses!" he cried. "Have done, and tell us the way to the gate."

At this moment a pair of mounted watchmen, hearing the din, turned their horses down the street. Seeing Sebastian and Isabel amid the urchins, and judging by Sebastian's clothing that he was a nobleman beset by rabble, they spurred their mounts, pulled out their truncheons, and galloped into the swarm, shouting:

"Never fear, your worship! We'll settle them for you! Away with you, little swine!"

Isabel, realizing the watchmen's blunder, cried out:

"There's no harm! Let them be!"

But her protests were drowned by the shrieking urchins, who scurried in all directions as the watchmen swung their truncheons. The housewives, having no mind to see their children's heads broken, now came bursting from the dwellings and threw themselves on the officers, who began clubbing right and left at anyone in reach.

To worsen matters, the beggar lurched into the alley. Brandishing his crutch, the huge fellow made straight for the crowd.

Seeing a double disaster overtaking them, Sebastian pulled Isabel close, plunged through the fracas, and took to his heels again, still with no idea where in all of Loringhold they could find a safe corner.

As they hastened on, the narrow street turned sharply

and widened into a marketplace where a tall clock-tower overlooked stands of vegetable sellers and fishmongers. The town gate lay directly ahead.

He ran toward it, but his glad cry changed to one of dismay. Instead of the pair of lazy-eyed watchmen he had expected, half-a-dozen dragoons, fully armed, were at the entry.

Impatient farmers and drovers jammed the gateway, some pushing to go out, others to go in, and all in such a tangle of carts, barrows, cows, sheep, and squawking poultry, that few succeeded in doing either. The guards, for their part, scanned the face of each traveler and rummaged through the vehicles.

Sebastian would have turned away, but he glimpsed the beggar, angrier and more determined than ever, hobble into the square.

Hoping the hunter had not sighted his prey, Sebastian hastily drew Isabel into the waiting crowd, judging it safer amid the livestock than among the passersby. By now, the throng had begun passing more quickly through the gate, and it was clear that he and Isabel, one moment or the next, must come under the sharp scrutiny of the guards.

Ahead of him, a farmer grumbled indignantly at the delay, and called out:

"What, then, do you mean to find lumps of gold in my swill barrel? Or the Captain turned into one of my pigs? Have done, and don't waste an honest fellow's time and temper."

"If you've nothing to hide, we've nothing to find," replied the guard. "Move along, now."

To speed the farmer on his way, the dragoon gave a

sound slap to the horse's flank. The wagon lurched ahead. The soldiers, however, had been at more pains to search the vehicle than to secure the railing that held the load of pigs, and these came tumbling out, squealing frantically, upsetting barrows and overturning baskets of geese as they bolted for freedom.

Sebastian seized the chance given by the farmer's misfortune. While the man tried to dash in all directions at once after his fleeing animals, berating guards and pigs in the same breath, Sebastian hastily thrust Isabel ahead of him. In another moment they darted through the gate, leaving the beggar, soldiers, tradesmen, geese, and pigs to settle matters among themselves.

Clear of the gate, he strode ahead with Isabel hurrying beside him.

"We're free of one trap, at least," he muttered to her, "and surely the worst. Step along, Princess, like the most carefree fellow in Loringhold, and never give a look behind."

As a coach-and-pair rattled by, the driver slowed his horse, leaned from the box, and called out:

"Hold, your honor, and tell me: Does the post road take me as quick as any to New Locking?"

"Why—why, I suppose it will," returned Sebastian, afraid to admit he was a stranger and had no idea where the town lay from the capital.

"If you're bound the same way, jump in," the coachman urged. "My master's sent me on a long errand. He'll be none the wiser if his coach is full or empty, and cost him no more, either."

Seeing his luck changing at last for the better, Sebastian gladly and gratefully opened the door, helped Isabel to clamber inside, and quickly followed her.

Within, a pair of hands flung him back against the seat. Sebastian stared into the smiling face of the barber.

xxv ∽ How Sebastian Rode in a Coach

As the Princess cried out in terror, Sebastian grappled with the barber, only to be seized by the throat and thrown heavily against the side of the coach.

Isabel fought wildly to free Sebastian, kicking, scratching, raining down blows on the barber with her two clenched fists. The coachman, however, leaped down from the box to join his fellow. In a trice, like men long used to their trade, the Regent's creatures had the fugitives bound and helpless.

The door snapped shut, the coach swung sharply around, and headed for the gate. It slowed a moment while the barber thrust out a red-sealed document, then plunged on recklessly through the crowd.

Drawing the blinds, the barber settled comfortably in his seat. Wearing green-tinted spectacles, and dressed now in a close-fitting black waistcoat and jacket with a spotless white neckcloth, he could have been taken for a notary or public scrivener.

In the half-light of the coach that had become a cell on four wheels, his spectacles glinted as he turned a glance on his prisoners, and bobbed his head briskly several times, delighted he had dispatched his task so neatly.

Sebastian struggled against his bonds, hardly thicker than threads but so cunningly knotted and looped that he succeeded only in tightening them. The Princess, though her face had gone ashen, raised her head and in her coldest regal tone commanded:

"Sir, we request and require you to set us at liberty. Any course other than immediate compliance with our direct and personal command will expose you to the severest consequences."

The barber first bowed his head apologetically, then hunched up his shoulders, and replied in his whining, fawning manner:

"Now, now, Your Grace, that I can't do, under the Regent's own command. A misfortunate situation; yes, I should say at least that. But surely Your Highness understands I could as well—how shall I put it?—have employed full discretionary alternatives. Oh yes, Your Grace, the Regent would have been equally glad to have Your Highness to the Glorietta alive or dead: in temporary or permanent suspension of vital faculties, as we rather think of it in our profession."

"You'd kill the Princess because the Regent ordered it?" cried Sebastian. "Obey a villain's command? You're as much a villain as Grinssorg himself."

"Am I, your worship?" replied the barber, distressed at this outburst. "I only follow my instructions. It's not for me to make the rights or wrongs of matters."

"Then free him," demanded Isabel. "He is a musician, and no point of contention between the Regent and ourselves."

The barber shook his head regretfully. "Alas, no, Your

Grace. I should expect the Regent will have to be the judge of that."

The coach at that moment lurched and swerved sharply, and for an instant Sebastian thought he might throw himself on the bloodhound and kick open the door on Isabel's side.

The barber, detecting his movement to do so, grinned crookedly at him and murmured:

"You'll not want to be playing tricks on me, your honor, will you? For I hope I'm as clever at my trade as your honor is at his own."

"Your trade? Butchery and bloodletting!" Sebastian flung back. "You cut the throat of that poor devil of an innkeeper in Darmstel, and you mean to do the same for us in Loringhold!"

The barber cringed a little and puckered his mouth in distaste:

"Please, your worship, there's no cause to take personal offense. Jugular severance, hematic diminution—proper and respected methods, no more than that. Alas, your honor has no appreciation of our difficulties. Then again, so few outside the profession do. The way of the world, I fear." He gave a little sigh, then added in a brisker tone, "But what a curious place the world is. A curious place indeed, wouldn't you agree, your honor? Now consider this: In Darmstel, I thought for certain you'd given me the slip. But when I came back to Loringhold, there's the two of you! Now, your worship, will you tell me that's not a cheerful turn of affairs? As I often observe, when all seems dimmest, there's sure to be a sunbeam to brighten the spirit."

Sebastian turned away and tried to shut his ears to the

bloodhound's repulsive chatter. Isabel was silent, not deigning to glance at her captor. The coach rattled on, gaining speed.

Until then, Presto had stayed quietly in the bottom of the bag. Now, adding to Sebastian's despair, the cat began working himself free of confinement, and in another moment hopped onto Sebastian's knees.

At the sight of Presto, the barber's cheerful expression turned to one of revulsion.

"What's this, what's this?" he exclaimed. "A cat? Ah, ah, that presumes too much on my good nature. Cats, indeed! Foul, treacherous creatures that they are! Sly, filthy beasts! Sickening, devious, disgusting! Into the gutter with you!"

So saying, he made to seize Presto, who bristled furiously, hissed, and bared his teeth. Determined to carry out his threat, heedless of his captive's enraged protests, the barber raised a hand to fetch the cat a stunning blow.

That instant, claws unsheathed, Presto sprang full upon the barber's chest.

The barber snatched him by the scruff of the neck and tore him away, though not before Presto had given his assailant's cheeks a good pair of scratches. The barber's fawning manner vanished. His face went livid and he spat out the most villainous curses, all the while tightening his stranglehold. Presto twisted and kicked his powerful hind legs, but his struggles to escape were as useless as those of his master to save him.

The barber's lips had frozen in a grimace. "Vicious beast! Well, my fine fellow, I'll have your claws out; and your eyes and your tail, while I'm at it!"

He hesitated a moment, seeing Sebastian thrashing

about in a last attempt to save his cat, and gave an icy laugh. A sly look came into the barber's eyes:

"Your worship so concerned? Well, your honor, you'll see a little of what we have in store for the likes of you."

He made a quick motion and a thin-bladed lancet dropped from his sleeve.

Sebastian, giving up any hope for escape, but seeing his beloved Duke of Gauli-Mauli about to share his fate, in a final effort heaved himself up and plunged headlong against the barber, who sent the lancet flying at him like a deadly dart. The struggles of Presto unsteadied the bloodhound's aim and the blade missed its mark, lodging in the side of the coach.

The barber flung aside the cat and turned to deal with Sebastian, at the same time shouting for his accomplice.

The coach pulled up to a sharp halt. The door burst open and a face thrust in. It was not the coachman Sebastian saw, but the beggar.

Within the instant, the huge fellow pulled Isabel from the vehicle, collared Sebastian, and sent him nearly tumbling to the cobbles of an empty street, his bag and fiddle along with him.

"Follow me!" shouted the beggar. "If you'd save your skin, use your legs!"

The barber snatched up his lancet, leaped out and made to plunge the weapon into Isabel's throat.

The beggar brought his crutch down heavily on the bloodhound's upraised arm, and the blade went spinning. Roaring in pain and fury at losing his victims and trying now to save his own skin, the barber scurried back to the coach, where Sebastian glimpsed the driver neatly gagged and trussed under the box. The frightened horses reared. Before the bloodhound could mount, the dangling reins whipped around him as the animals bolted, dragging the shrieking assassin with them.

The beggar, meantime, had cut the fugitives' bonds. Without waiting to see more or ask further, Sebastian caught up his bag and raced where his rescuer led, with Isabel half-carried between them and Presto speeding along beside, dodging and turning through such a maze of alleys and passageways that he lost track altogether of where they were going.

At last, the beggar hustled his charges down a narrow flight of wooden steps, into a cellar lined with vats and barrels, through one low doorway, then another, into a drab chamber, lit by a single guttering candle. There he finally allowed the fugitives to halt and catch their breath.

"I'd have brought you closer than this, and saved you some hasty steps," declared the beggar as Sebastian stared around him. "The coachman was glad enough to do my bidding, all the more with my knife tickling his ribs.

"I feared I'd lost you at the gate," he went on. "For all that, you led me a merry chase, and if that rogue's coach hadn't slowed when it did, I'd still be playing hare and hounds." He laughed and rubbed his shoulders. "As for you, Princess Isabel, if you give alms as freely as you give cudgelings, the beggars of Loringhold will all be rich."

"Sir, who are you and where have you taken us?" Isabel replied. "We demand to be given this information directly."

"You're in the safest place in Loringhold," said the beggar. "For you, very likely the only safe one."

"The washerwoman's doing!" Sebastian exclaimed. "And I thought for certain she betrayed us."

The beggar grinned. "She did, after a fashion. And rightly so. But never fear, we'll harm neither of you. As for what else we do—that must wait on the Captain to settle."

THE Captain? In Loringhold? Here? What will he do
with us?" Though he had a dozen more questions, Sebastian saw from the beggar's expression that asking them
would be a waste of breath. The most he learned was the
fellow's name: Benno. Beyond that, the beggar refused to
tell more.

"What you're to know or not know depends on the
Captain," Benno said. "Meantime, you can both be
thankful you're not in that bloodhound's coach."

The beggar, though beggar clearly he was not, then
promised food would soon be brought. He addressed his
captives good-naturedly and with a rough kindness, but
after he left the cellar the Princess looked more troubled
than before.

"While our demise has been held momentarily in
abeyance, we are nonetheless incarcerated—we mean,
we're alive but still prisoners."

Sebastian nodded. "When I think how I wanted to
join the Captain—well, now I have! But I never imagined he'd be our jailer!"

"Or executioner," Isabel said calmly.

"Ah, no!" Sebastian assured her. "Benno said you'd come to no harm." He stopped; from all that had happened, he realized there was no reason to trust the beggar more than the barber.

If the same distressing thought had come to Isabel, her face and voice gave no sign of it. Instead, she began stroking Presto, who had hopped onto her knees. She did not look at Sebastian as she said:

"If you meant once to join the Captain, you may join him yet. When he learns you want to follow him, he'll surely spare your life."

"And let him take yours? Now, Princess, you do me an injustice. I may be only a fiddler, but even a fiddler wouldn't forsake his—" He hesitated, then as lightly as he could, he declared: "Why, he'd not forsake the finest dancer in the Gallimaufry-Theatricus!"

Despite this attempt to put Isabel in better spirits, she turned away without answering. And, as the day passed, Sebastian began privately to fear their plight was more dangerous than at first he had imagined.

Benno was good as his word insofar as the food he promised did arrive. It was ample, well prepared, and brought by none other than the washerwoman. Her gruff manner had changed to fond concern, and she declared herself willing to see to all of Isabel's needs. But once, as the door was briefly opened, Sebastian glimpsed a large room beyond their prison. Bigger than a merchant's storage cellar, it was filled with stacks of pikes and sabers.

"The Captain's own stronghold, in the middle of Loringhold?" Sebastian whispered. "It must be. Now, there's a secret that few in Hamelin-Loring know." He did not, however, add his doubts about how long he or the Princess would be allowed to keep that knowledge.

Isabel had withdrawn into her own thoughts. The washerwoman had offered her a coarse shawl, for the cellar was damp and chill. The Princess accepted it as if it had been royal ermine, and sat quietly at the wooden table, clasping the shabby garment about her shoulders. Watching her, Sebastian remembered wondering whether Isabel's plan to lead an army had been nothing more than a wild and witless notion. Now, he believed beyond question she had strength and spirit to do it. Once, he had laughed at her for her solemn ways and elaborate declamations. But these seemed to burn away in the light of the guttering candle; and he saw no courtly puppet, but a girl whose grace made a threadbare shawl more beautiful than the glittering costume of the Gallimaufry-Theatricus.

He went to her and took her hand. "So far, I've done badly for you. You could hardly have fared worse if we'd never met. But I'll give you my word—indeed, I'll give whatever else is needed—you'll have your throne again."

Isabel smiled sadly. "Once, that would have been important to us. Our devoted subjects? We've seen more truth about them in a child's game than all the Regent's councillors ever told us. Our subjects? Yes, but not of their own choice. Devoted? Yes, though not to us."

"Come now," Sebastian replied as cheerfully as he could, "don't belittle one that's both a subject and devoted." Imitating Quicksilver's grandest manner, he bowed deeply. "The famous clown, late of the world-renowned Gallimaufry-Theatricus, and now your obedient servant. And not to overlook still another: His Most Exalted Catliness, the Duke of Gauli-Mauli himself!"

The Princess lowered her eyes and her smile was shadowed. "We should be happy if all our kingdom consisted only of those two."

"And so should I," Sebastian began.

Isabel turned quickly away and, with some difficulty reassumed her courtly speech, saying:

"On one point all our Councillors-Royal agreed: That personal affection must never influence a sovereign; indeed, that it must never even be felt." Her eyes filled with tears and she burst out: "Were they right? Was this another lie told us as truth? May not a Princess answer her heart and give it where she chooses?"

"Quicksilver told me of a play they put on in the Theatricus," Sebastian murmured. "A swineherd who loved a princess. No more than a nursery tale. Yet he told me those who saw it believed it, even knowing it was moonshine. But why should it be only that? Why should it not happen in truth?"

Isabel did not reply, and Sebastian himself dared say nothing further.

The door had opened quietly meanwhile, and Sebastian turned, expecting to see Benno or the washerwoman. He blinked at the figure in the candlelight, at first unable to make out the features. In another moment he gave a shout of amazement.

It was Nicholas.

The stout traveler was hardly as jaunty as when Sebastian first met him. His clothing was creased, disheveled, and dusty; grime streaked his plump cheeks, and his sparse hair hung damp on his brow.

Sebastian ran to him. "Nicholas! It's our good fortune but, alas, not yours. Why have they brought you here? My poor friend, what's gone amiss with you? As for us, we're the Captain's prisoners. But we've been waiting so long for him I could almost think he's neither dark nor fair, light nor swarthy, but more rumor than reality, and there's no such person at all!"

"There is, that I assure you," Nicholas replied. "Andreas found him, as I knew he would." He gave Sebastian and Isabel a shy grin, and drew a long breath that was half a sigh and half a bemused chuckle.

"Yes, he could hardly fail to do so," Nicholas added. "You see, the Captain—well, in point of fact, and in a manner of speaking, I should have to say: I'm the Captain."

XXVII   How Nicholas Told His Trade

SEBASTIAN had pulled up a chair for Nicholas, but these words took him so aback that he sat down on it himself.

"The Captain?" he stammered. "You? But Andreas said— But what of the great strapping fellow, and eyes like lightning, and tall as a tree—?"

Nicholas puffed out his cheeks, cleared his throat in embarrassment, and apologetically replied:

"Ah—as for that, none of my doing, you can be sure. Tongues wag, one thing piles on top of another. And all the more, as most of the Captain's staunchest followers have never seen him. But if it suits them to match him to their fancy, if it pleases them to believe he's dark or fair, tall or short, I daresay there's no harm one way or the other. I'd even call it a blessing, since I can't be everywhere at once and it speeds my work for me. Good fellows like Andreas—if I myself can't reach these folk to rally them against Grinssorg, likely as not they end up doing their own deeds; and bolder than my reputed ones! There must be a hundred Captains in Hamelin-Loring, men and women both. I should even say, in a manner of speaking, that anyone who does his part for a measure of justice in the Principality—why, he himself is the Captain, without even knowing it."

"A cook, a piper, a tailor, and likely a dozen others besides," Sebastian murmured. "And your true trade none of them—"

"Or all of them, if you'd see it that way," said Nicholas. "What better guise, these days, than every guise?

"And you, Princess," he went on, briskly and cheerily, "you can imagine it's a relief to find you safe. After we fought our way clear of the soldiers, I managed at last to pick up your trail as far as Great Brunswick. By then, I was too late. The pair of you were beyond anyone's help. Benno, luckily, was able to get word to me; though all he could tell was that the Princess and a fiddler had somehow blundered their way into Loringhold. He never knew I had the honor of your previous acquaintance."

At the first appearance of Nicholas, Isabel had been as glad as Sebastian was to see him. Now she drew coldly away, saying:

"Sir, the accounts of the Captain which we received from our ministers of state, depicting you as an ill-favored brigand no longer coincide with the evidence here presented and directly discernible to us. Although we have confidence in your courtesy toward our person, we do not presume further assistance in our cause from one inimical to our Royal House—or, as we have learned to put it more simply: we can't expect help from our sworn enemy."

"Enemy?" replied Nicholas, puzzled and dismayed. "Of Grinssorg, yes, but not of Princess Isabel. The Captain —or Captains, I should say—have no thought of over-

turning the Royal House. Someday the monarchy may
wear out its usefulness and fade of its own accord. But
until then—the folk of Hamelin-Loring are still too used
to monarchs, they'd be ill at ease without one. No, Princess, it's not your monarchy we fight against but the Regent's tyranny. Nothing would please me more than to
see you take the throne in your own right. But you can't
do it if you're dead! As you'll surely be if Grinssorg has
his way. Indeed, ever since I learned you'd left the Glorietta I've been looking for you, hoping to keep you out
of harm. When I found you at last, and you told me you
were going to Upper Cassel, I wanted only to speed you
safely on your way."

Isabel looked at him in astonishment. "You knew that
we fled the palace? How—"

Nicholas grinned at her. "Your Chief Groom is one of
the Captain's good men. I had word from him almost the
moment you set foot outside the Glorietta."

"But, Nicholas," Sebastian broke in, "if the Captain
has rallied men to his cause, Isabel has no need of Prince
Frederick's army. You yourself must have an army of
your own followers, ready and waiting to destroy the Regent."

Nicholas ruefully shook his head. "Still too few and
still too weak. I'd not dare a trial of strength against the
Regent yet. One day it will come to that. But not now. It
would cost lives to no purpose. As for Prince Frederick,
that's a question whether he'd help in the first place. And
if he did, whether he'd be willing to take his leave afterward. It's often the way of princes to outstay their invita-
tions. In any case, the Princess will be safer in her uncle's

court than in her own. I'll see to it that she reaches Upper Cassel."

Isabel did not reply for some moments. When at last she did, her voice was still troubled:

"Captain Nicholas, the veracity of your remarks is unquestioned," she began, hesitated, then went on quickly. "We believe you're telling the truth. But what of ourselves? Can we do nothing better than live in exile? We've seen a grape grower robbed of his land; a washerwoman left without husband or brother. Even an urchin girl who wept at playing Princess Isabel in a child's game. Small cares to you, perhaps, but painful to us. Is there nothing you wish for Hamelin-Loring that we ourselves would not also wish?"

"Ah, Princess, we ask far more than the Regent would grant," answered Nicholas. "We'll give you our allegiance, but at the same time we want no less than a Grand Council, so that all in Hamelin-Loring, high or low, shall have their voices heard and their wants known."

"You've given us your good will," said Isabel. "Take our promise in return. If we ever regain our throne, you shall have the Grand Council that you want."

"All I want at the moment is your safety," said Nicholas. "I urge you to stay in Upper Cassel until the Captain and his men are strong enough to unseat the Regent. When that's done, we'll welcome you back to your realm."

Sebastian quickly took Isabel's hand and said to her:

"You'll not journey alone, not if you'll have a fiddler for company."

Isabel blushed and nodded. "We'll journey nowhere without you."

Nicholas gave Sebastian and Isabel a quick, appraising glance. "I'm glad to hear you both agree. But you, Sebastian, have little choice in the matter. You've been seen too much in Loringhold. You're a peril to yourself and all of us. Why, the Regent would give half the realm and count it cheap to know as much as you've learned here."

He clapped his hands in a brisk and businesslike manner. "Now then, the two of you, we'll set our plans and you'll soon be on your way."

XXVIII ❧ How Sebastian
Was Betrayed

$\mathcal{H}$AVING learned that the mild-mannered Nicholas, with his cherub's face and air of perplexed innocence, was in fact the bold and daring Captain, Sebastian was sure nothing more could astonish him.

"If he told us we were to escape in Grinssorg's own carriage," he told Isabel, "I'd take it as the most ordinary thing in the world—even if he set Presto up as the coachman."

However, once again Nicholas surprised them.

"I'll not risk sending you through Hamelin-Loring," he said. "No, you'll reach Upper Cassel on a road smoother than the Royal Highway."

Sebastian soon understood his friend's intention when Benno arrived, shortly afterward, with a bundle of sailor's garments.

"There's a ship in Loring Harbor, sailing with the tide for Cassel Haven," said Nicholas. "The master vows he'll not be curious about a couple of passengers. But the port's closely guarded, so you'd best wear these. The Princess will do nicely as a cabin boy; the fiddler, a deckhand. And Presto—why, no vessel would sail without a ship's cat. Benno and I will see you safely aboard. Then we'll say our farewells and hope we'll meet again, for the Captain has his own tasks to do."

Some while before dawn, the voyagers clambered into a cart driven by Benno, and set off for the port; not through the town gates, but along the riverside quays, which soon grew crowded with warehouses, ship's chandlers, storage sheds, and piles of cargo ready for loading.

Isabel huddled in a sea-cloak, for the air was chill with mist. Presto crouched on Sebastian's knees. Nicholas, with a broad-brimmed hat shadowing his face, sat calmly beside Benno.

Detachments of soldiers were stationed about the docks. Benno, therefore, left the cart amid a stand of barrels and a heap of sacks, where it would draw no attention. With Presto as usual on Sebastian's shoulder, the band now went afoot toward the piers, approaching the last obstacle to their journey: a tollhouse and customs shed manned by a couple of sleepy port watchmen.

Nicholas ordered all to be in good spirits and a little boisterous, to seem a company of sailors returning to their ship, and he himself began whistling through his teeth. He called out a few seafarers' jests to the port watchmen; the officers replied in kind, and showed no inclination to trouble themselves over a party of shipmates.

"Along with you, before the tide starts running," one of the officers told Sebastian. "But look sharp for stowaways. There's talk of a couple rogues that might be glad enough to put some water between themselves and the law. As for that sack of yours," he added, jokingly, "has one of those villains crept into it and hid there?" He laughed and gave the bag a good-natured poke with his staff.

The watchman's gesture set the fiddle a-jangling, and the stroke of his staff echoed from the instrument. He frowned, and raised his lantern to shine on Sebastian.

"What knocks hollow in there? It's got a funny ring."

Squinting closer, he glimpsed the neck and carved head on the scroll of the violin, and put out his hand to touch it. "Here, that's an odd thing."

Nicholas and Benno halted and drew close beside Isabel. Sebastian felt his heart leap into his mouth and he stammered:

"Why—why, no more than a fiddle. To liven the voyage and keep the ship's company in good spirit."

"A fiddle, plain enough," the officer returned, "but like none I've ever seen. Let's have a look, you sea-ape."

The bland smile had not left the face of Nicholas, though now it seemed fixed and frozen. The officer beckoned to his comrade, saying:

"Here, Fallstick, you've an eye for such things. What do you make of this? A handsome piece to find in a sea-urchin's bag?"

Despite Sebastian's protests, the man called Fallstick pulled fiddle and bow from the bag, examined the instrument closely, and muttered to his colleague:

"I make it to be worth more ducats than you and I could hope to jingle in a lifetime."

He turned to Sebastian and demanded:

"How did you come by this? You never bought it. Where did you steal it, you villain?"

"Not stolen," Sebastian declared, reaching for the fiddle. "A gift—"

"Given?" cried Fallstick, holding the instrument beyond Sebastian's grasp. "Ah, now, we're not babes in the woods. This? Given? To the likes of you?"

"Now, sir," Nicholas put in, courteously doffing his hat, "you'll not delay us, so that we have to go swimming after our berths? It's true, as my mate says."

"Slowly, slowly," warned Fallstick. "There's a smell that warrants a little more sniffing." He motioned with his head toward the tollhouse. "A gift, eh? Well, I wish somebody made me such a gift. I'd waste no time selling it. And that's what you mean to do, isn't it, you thief?"

"No!" Sebastian cried. "I'd never sell it. There's not enough money in all Hamelin-Loring—"

"Aha," returned Fallstick, on the heels of Sebastian's outburst. "You admit the thing has value, do you?"

He looked sharply at Sebastian. "There's a bit of the truth," he went on, turning the fiddle slowly in his hands. "We'll have all of it soon. Oh yes, you'll be anchored a while with us. And your shipmates, too."

So saying, he drew a pistol from his belt and pointed it at the fugitives.

Sebastian glanced despairingly at Isabel and Nicholas. His sailor's garb felt drenched in cold seawater. The sight of his beloved violin in the hands of Fallstick turned him sick at heart. He hesitated, his eyes on the instrument whose like, he knew, he would never find again. The music the fiddle had brought him sang through his head, but he tried to shut his ears to it. He straightened, took a deep breath, as if he were about to step onto the stage of Quicksilver's Gallimaufry-Theatricus, and said lightly and offhandedly:

"Now, I'm not one to stir trouble for myself or my mates. Whatever you claim the fiddle's worth, I set little store by the thing. Since it cost me nothing in the first place, I could hardly suffer from the loss, could I? Now, if you were to keep that worthless fiddle, you'd have no reason to keep us—"

Fallstick's comrade pursed his lips. "That might put a prettier face on the matter."

"You're a fool," interrupted Fallstick. "I call that fiddle contraband, and ours by right of seizure. For the rest of these gallows birds, who knows there's not a reward for netting them? We could profit at both ends. Let's have these fellows behind bars, first; then see how matters stand."

XXIX ✑ How Sebastian Ran a Race

NICHOLAS was the first to move. Quicker than Sebastian's eyes could follow, Nicholas swept his broad-brimmed hat like a lash across the face of Fallstick.

The watchman stumbled back a pace, and his pistol fired harmlessly in the air. Nicholas was upon his opponent within the instant. At the same time, Benno grappled Fallstick's comrade and with a stunning blow of his huge fist sent him sprawling to the cobbles.

"Follow me!" cried Nicholas, seizing Isabel's arm and setting off with all haste down the dockside.

The pistol shot, however, had brought a detachment of soldiers on the double to the far end of the pier. Before they could glimpse the fugitives, Nicholas changed his course and plunged into the shadows of a stand of barrels, Presto darting beside him.

The soldiers, by now, had come upon the two unconscious watchmen. An officer shouted a command and Sebastian heard the troop go clattering along the dock.

Nicholas hurriedly picked his way among the piles of barrels. Sebastian, to his dismay, realized a long stretch of open pier lay ahead, and they dared not cross it without being seen.

The soldiers, meanwhile, had begun searching through the stacks of cargo. Although Nicholas led the fugitives from one hiding place to the next, striving always to keep hidden, he now stopped and turned back. The little man showed no sign of losing heart, but Sebastian saw all too clearly that he was hemmed in and effectively trapped no matter which way he turned.

Benno's face was grim. "Small hope, four together. Shall we make a run for it, no matter?"

Nicholas shook his head. "Hold a while. They may still pass us by."

The fugitives crouched silently in the darkness. For a moment, Sebastian's hopes rose as the soldiers appeared to give up their search and regroup on the pier. But, from what he could make out, they had no intention of leaving the dockside. Instead, he heard an order for lanterns to be brought and the hunt to be pressed more closely.

Nicholas grinned bitterly. "Alas, the Captain can't do all the marvels they claim." He glanced at Benno, and said in a very matter-of-fact way, "But one thing's certain: the Captain won't be taken alive."

"Captain Nicholas," Isabel said quietly, "we asked only for your help, not your life." She turned to Sebastian. "Nor that of anyone in our—in our esteem. The Regent seeks the Princess of Hamelin-Loring. Let him find her."

With that, Isabel made to climb to her feet.

Sebastian hastily pulled the girl back into the protecting shadows.

"Nicholas," he demanded, "if the way's clear, can you still help Isabel reach the ship?"

Nicholas nodded. "A chance—"

"Take it, then," Sebastian said, and heedless of Isabel's outcry he sprang from the shelter of the cargo, plunged through the ranks of barrels, and raced to the pier.

Sighting him instantly, the soldiers streamed after their fleeing quarry. Not daring a backward glance, hoping only that his ruse would trick them long enough, he dodged and darted among the sacks, vats, and boxes along the wharf, leading his pursuers farther from the harbor.

Musketry rattled behind him. He flung himself to the cobbles, then scrambled up and stumbled ahead. All the troop had now taken up the chase, determined their prey this time would not escape.

As he sped along the quayside, for a moment he believed he had outdistanced them, and might hope for his own freedom as well as Isabel's. He swung around a corner. Ahead, lantern in hand, stood a figure in a grimy pair of canvas trousers and the coarse jacket of a seaman.

It was the barber.

The bloodhound quickly set down his lantern; and Sebastian, before he could slow his pace or turn back, ran headlong into his clutches.

Sebastian fought to break loose from the grip of the barber, who pulled a sailor's dirk from his belt. Sebastian twisted aside as the point of the blade ripped through his shirt, and threw himself backward to send the barber tumbling to the cobbles along with him.

Cursing, the bloodhound rolled aside and raised his arm to strike again. The lantern was by Sebastian's hand.

He snatched it up, and threw it straight at his assailant's head.

The barber screamed horribly as the glass shattered and flame caught his hair. He stumbled back, head blazing like a torch, and toppled from the quay.

Sebastian jumped to his feet and set off again. But he had reckoned without the bloodhound's accomplice. The false coachman, hurrying to join his fellow, burst from the shadows and seized him by the throat.

Though Sebastian fought with all his strength, the soldiers pouring onto the quay were upon him in an instant.

HE cell where Sebastian found himself was hardly bigger than some of the cages in Baron Purn-Hessel's aviary. He sank down in a corner and put his battered face in his hands. The soldiers had beaten him so mercilessly that he scarcely remembered being trussed up and bundled into some sort of cart, dragged and prodded down flights of steps, and at last flung behind the bars of this cubicle. This much he knew, and nothing more: He was in the Glorietta.

Isabel, Nicholas, Presto—his fears for their safety tormented him more than his abuse at the hands of his captors. His doubts and hopes were all so mixed he could not sort one from another. Along with them, the maddest thoughts went skittering through his head: the Glorietta —Isabel had lived all her life there, and he wondered if she had any notion such a prison lay at the bottom of it. And Quicksilver declaring his new fiddler would travel all the way to the palace.

"And so I have!" Sebastian thought, groaning miserably and laughing half-hysterically at the same time. "And here I am! And surely the first and last time I'll ever see it!"

A gross figure in a dazzling waistcoat had come to stand before the bars. For an instant, Sebastian was sure this apparition had no more substance than the rest of his disordered memories.

"The Purse?" he murmured. "That tub of lard, even here? Now for sure I'm having a nightmare."

But the fat courtier was altogether real and he stared at Sebastian in disgust, hardly able to bring himself to exchange so much as a word with such a befouled, bedraggled creature. His jowls twitched, his nose wrinkled, but at last he said in a cold voice:

"Now then, you villain, the Regent means to know the whereabouts of Princess Isabel, and you shall tell me that on the instant."

This question from The Purse gave Sebastian the brightest glimmer of hope since his capture. If Isabel and Nicholas had not been taken, if truly they were still alive, then perhaps they had made good their escape.

"Why, Excellency," he exclaimed gladly, "that I don't know."

"Young liar," The Purse replied. "The Regent is fully cognizant of your actions on her behalf. Yours, and those of still another scoundrel. Yes, the Regent shall know more of him, too. Speak up, now. Quick. Who are you? What's your game in all this matter?"

"As for who I am," Sebastian answered boldly, "Your Excellency should know that as well as anyone."

"What?" cried The Purse. "Insolent rogue! You dare claim acquaintance with me?"

"It was you, indeed, who cost me my place," returned Sebastian, grinning despite himself at the look of shock on the courtier's face. "You've not forgotten the day you thought your breeches torn? The fiddler in Baron Purn-Hessel's orchestra—"

The Purse stared blankly at him. "I recall no such incident, nor conceive any circumstances in which you could have figured. You? In Baron Purn-Hessel's service? That much can be very promptly determined."

Drawing aside, The Purse summoned a jailer from the end of the corridor, spoke apart with him for a moment, then returned to set his great bulk on a chair, from which he glanced disdainfully at Sebastian.

Sebastian's spirits rose higher. He was sure now that Isabel was safely away, and the true identity of Nicholas still unknown.

"My poor lad!"

Sebastian looked up in surprise, and jumped to his feet. At the bars of the cell stood Baron Purn-Hessel himself.

For all his splendid attire, the nobleman's face seemed grayer and wearier than Sebastian remembered it. More astonishing was the distress in the Baron's voice as he went on:

"Sebastian! Unhappy fellow, what's brought you to such a pass? Count Lobelieze told me nothing—"

"What, then, Purn-Hessel, this fellow *was* in your service?" The Purse broke in. "You should know, sir, your fiddler has information the Regent requires without delay. A stubborn rogue, but he shall be dealt with."

"Let me speak with him, Count," requested the Baron. "If you would leave us to ourselves a moment."

The Purse shrugged and stepped away. The Baron turned hastily to Sebastian. Instead of upbraiding him, he spoke gently and with great concern:

"Ah, my lad, if the Regent has a hand in this, you're in deeper trouble than you ever could imagine. If only you'd stayed with me and not run off as you did—"

"Run off?" Sebastian replied, astonished. He laughed bitterly. "Why, Excellency, The Purse has forgotten— and so have you. You were the one who sent me on my way."

"I remember all too well," said the Baron. "With Count Lobelieze in such a rage, I could have done nothing else at the time. But I never expected you to heed me! Rascal that you were, you'd never taken pains to obey me before! I was sure you'd stay out of sight until the matter cooled. But no! The one time you chose to follow my orders to the letter! And even so, did you think, in any case, I'd have sent you off poorer than a beggar? You were a fine fiddler, for all that you were a scamp—and doubtless still are. More than that, I was fond of you— and still am."

The Baron shook his head as he continued:

"Alas, the misunderstanding was yours, but the fault was mine, and you have been on my conscience more than a little. If I'm to make up the sum the Regent demands, I shall be scarcely better off than you. Indeed, you've made me think that if I had stood against the Regent from the first, none of this would have happened. I've learned that to my sorrow. A costly lesson. Almost as costly as yours. But, my boy, what more mischief have you done? If it's anything to do with the disappearance of Princess Isabel, speak out with all you know. My word upon it, I'll see the Regent deals leniently with you. And your place—I never meant for you to lose it. You'll have it back again, and everything will be as it was."

Hearing these last words, for an instant Sebastian could fancy that the Cook was still saving a cup of chocolate for him; that the Serving Maids were still pining away for him; and that he needed only to nod his head to find himself back in a world happier than all the rest of Hamelin-Loring.

"As it was?" he murmured. His thoughts turned to Isabel and Nicholas; and in his mind's ear he heard Lelio's fiddle. "My place? No, it is truly lost."

"Have done, Purn-Hessel," The Purse broke in. "You should know there's only one way to deal with such a rogue."

As the Baron turned reluctantly away, The Purse fixed Sebastian with a severe eye:

"Play no more games with me, you wretch. Where is the Princess?"

"Shall I tell you that?" Sebastian exclaimed. "Very well, you'll know this much: By now, she's far out of reach. Carry that to your master, with a fiddler's compliments."

"Impudent whelp," replied The Purse, "do you take us all for fools like you? The Regent has already surmised that you conspired to have her taken aboard a ship. Your plan failed, my fine fiddler. The Princess and your accomplice are still in Loringhold."

Sebastian gasped in dismay as The Purse continued:

"You can protect her no longer. She is as much an outlaw as you are. The Regent has declared her flight equal to her abdication. Any attempt on her part to regain the throne, and any attempt to help her do so shall be construed as treason, punishable by death. There is no longer a Princess of Hamelin-Loring. The Regent has commanded the highest state occasion for this night—when he shall proclaim himself Prince of the Realm."

Sebastian gripped the bars of his cell to keep himself from falling. Though his hopes for Isabel's safety were shattered, he prayed that Nicholas and Benno would strike on some other plan. In any case, only his silence could protect her. He raised his head and answered as boldly as he could.

"Then, Excellency, your master's first princely act must be to hang a fiddler, for he'll hear no more from me than what I've said. Unless he'd care to have me play a tune for him."

"Hang?" replied The Purse. He smiled for the first time; and Sebastian, who had taken the courtier for no more than a gross buffoon, saw that the man's face hid a terrifying cruelty. "You shall beg to hang before certain gentlemen finish with you. They are, as I'm told, excellent at their trade. I suggest they might have your fingers off, one by one. Do you claim to be a fiddler? I doubt you shall be one for long. Surely not beyond this midnight."

XXXI ❧ How Sebastian Was Remembered

THE Purse had gone. In the corner of the cell, Sebastian crouched with his knees drawn up and his arms wrapped about them, shuddering more from his fearful imaginings than from the dampness of his prison; unsure whether he was awake and dreaming himself asleep; or asleep and dreaming himself awake. Worse, he could no longer reckon the time. The only light came from the jailer's post at the end of the corridor, and it trickled through his cage in a cold gray streak.

The tramp of hobnailed boots brought him to his feet, trembling violently but nevertheless vowing to face his torturers as best he could.

The bars rattled open. Instead of seizing him, the guards flung another prisoner into the cell. Propelled by a booted foot, the new captive went tumbling headlong against the wall, rolled himself upright, and began shouting all manner of abuse and protest after the departing jailers.

"Scoundrels! Knaves! Pigs! You'll not treat a man of my reputation like this!"

"Quicksilver!" Sebastian cried, hurrying to the side of the impresario. "You? A prisoner?"

"What else?" replied Quicksilver, nodding ruefully. His gaudy costume was ripped and begrimed, his waistcoat torn down the front, and his glorious mustache drooped pitifully. Now that the guards had gone, his show of bravado vanished and he slumped crestfallen and wretched as Sebastian himself.

"Colleagues in art, now companions in misery," declared Quicksilver, after Sebastian told him of the balloon flight, its consequences, and as much about Nicholas as he judged safe for the impresario to know.

"Fortunately," said Quicksilver, "the ravishing Madame Sophie, that delicate flower of grace, was able to make a run for it, along with Adam and Winkler, while the dastardly minions of the law were held at bay by your obedient servant.

"At the end, alas, I succumbed, and those two yokels hauled me to the magistrate. But as soon as the magistrate heard Princess Isabel might be involved, he packed me off to his superior, who then packed me off to his. By that time, one of the Regent's bloodhounds sniffed something fishy in the matter, and I was whisked away in a closed coach at full gallop, with never a stop until we reached Loringhold, this very moment past.

"As for that villain, Flasch," Quicksilver added, with a laugh of sour satisfaction, "the magistrate had him marched off to prison, where I hope he spends the rest of his days. The judge had no mind to blame his own officers, so instead he accused Flasch of letting you escape! And had him locked up straightaway!"

"In prison as he deserves—but for the wrong reason," Sebastian replied, shaking his head. "Scoundrel he is, but I'm sorry for him. He must feel as I did when I lost my place. The Purse had me thrown out—and doesn't even remember me. The Baron didn't mean to send me away —but away I went. And all for a pair of torn breeches that were never torn to begin with. Yet see where those breeches led all of us! Ah, Quicksilver, is it the truth of the matter that counts? Or the matter of the truth as folk choose to see it? Or is anything at all as it seems?"

"Not always, my boy," Quicksilver admitted. "Sometimes, indeed, things are worse than they look. But—just as often, they're better."

"Yes," replied Sebastian, "the Merry Host in Dorn turned out to be the sourest fellow in the world. And my friend Nicholas, who seemed as mild as milk, was the bravest man I've known. The world's a strange business, Quicksilver, with as much hoaxing in it as the Gallimaufry-Theatricus."

"Not so!" cried the impresario. "One thing, at least, we never do in the Theatricus: We never hoax ourselves! No, I'm well aware our swords are wooden, our diamonds glass. And I—no better than a traveling tinker. Even the delightful Thornless Rose is, ah, shall we say, a little past her prime. But that makes no difference. What's important? The Theatricus? No. It's the folk who come to watch us. They see themselves brave, strong, beautiful! And why? Because somewhere in their hearts that's what they are! Make-believe and moonshine? No! We show them only the truth—as it might be."

"What of a fiddler?" Sebastian answered. "I didn't believe you when you told me Lelio's violin would only play for a worthy master. Did I have it in myself to be a true musician? And never knew it? The fiddle's brought me to grief, and all of us. I'm sure if it hadn't been for the fiddle, we'd have been safe away. I wish Presto had never found it, that you'd never given it to me. And yet —and yet, I'd still give all I have to hear its music again."

"I'm afraid, my boy," Quicksilver glumly replied, "we're both beyond wishing one thing or the other."

Sebastian nodded. "If I could have been a true musician, I've learned it too late. The fiddle's gone. There's as much chance of finding it as there is of my helping Isabel. Well, at least I can dream myself the swineherd in love with a princess. For I do love her, Quicksilver, and I believe she loves me. Do you remember when you took us for a runaway couple? I laughed at you. But you saw the truth of it clearer than I did. And now—it can be no more than a dream."

He was silent a long moment, then turned to the impresario. "Quicksilver, what's the time? Tell me, for mercy, what hour is it?"

"Time?" The impresario shrugged. "What's either of us to be concerned with time? Furthermore, I don't know. Those swine robbed me of my watch, into the bargain. But I should say close on to midnight."

Hearing this, Sebastian groaned in despair.

"Whatever shall I do? The Purse said I was to be tortured, and for that I trust him to keep his word. But, Quicksilver, I'm not as brave as Nicholas. I fear it with all my heart, and I've no strength for it. To show myself a coward—that makes no difference to me, for there's nothing I can win or lose now by pretending one thing or the other. But alas, that's no help to Isabel. How shall I be brave? Not for myself, but for her?"

Quicksilver shook his head. "Put on as bold a face as you can, my boy, as I've seen players brazen out a poor performance in the Gallimaufry-Theatricus."

"Fancy myself brave?" Sebastian grinned at him. "If a swineherd could slay a dragon, I'll take it for my own example. Shall I do less than the hero of a nursery tale? Yes, I'll dream myself brave and take heart from it! And better than that. Indeed, I'll fancy myself not in prison at all! Come along, my friend, let's have a picnic!"

Quicksilver blinked as Sebastian, briskly clapping his hands, squatted cross-legged on the stones and went through the motions of opening a hamper and spreading out a tablecloth.

"Here's an excellent bottle," Sebastian cried, making a show of drawing the cork. "And what's this? A cold fowl! More than enough for all of us. They're waiting for us, Quicksilver, all those we love. Madame Sophie should be along to greet you soon. And for me—Isabel, Nicholas, and my dear Duke of Gauli-Mauli, all waiting for me just around the corner! Now, a song to put all right!"

Quicksilver, falling in with the game, joined his voice to Sebastian's, and soon they were singing gaily, all manner of part-songs, rounds, catches, and glees, laughing with delight at their own harmonies, and never stopping until they were out of breath.

"A splendid wine!" cried Quicksilver. "You'll not find as good a bottle at any vintner's!"

"And the fowl well roasted!" Sebastian answered. "Done to a turn! Why, fancy's the best relish for any dish!"

Both were quiet then. For those moments, Sebastian's heart lifted a little and he forgot his anguish. As refreshed as if he had in truth shared a bottle with Quicksilver, he strove to compose his thoughts and cling to the strength he had gained.

By now he was sure his time must soon be upon him. He strained his ears for any sound of bells tolling the hour. Drawing a deep breath, gritting his teeth against whatever lay in store for him, he climbed restlessly to his feet.

A shadow flickered along the corridor. Sebastian rubbed his eyes, which were surely playing tricks on him. Then he gasped in disbelief.

XXXII ⟡ How Sebastian
Found a Place

RESTO!" The cat sprang into his arms, and Sebastian sank his cheek against Presto's fur.

"Your Catliness! Duke of Gauli-Mauli! How did you get here? Isabel . . . Nicholas. . . . If you could only tell me! But what have you done? Run off? Lost them? Or have they lost you?"

"He's a bold creature, no matter what," Quicksilver declared. "I wish we were as thin as he, to creep through these bars."

"He's followed me for the last time," Sebastian replied, sadly stroking the cat. "We'll soon part. Farewell, Presto. You never got the pillow and saucer I promised. But I know you'll make your way in Loringhold better than your master did."

He stopped and put a hand to Presto's throat. "What's this? Were you tied up? Here's a cord. And this—"

He caught his breath. Another cord had been looped around the cat's breast. Between this makeshift harness hung a long piece of metal.

"A key!" Sebastian hurriedly untied the strings. "From Nicholas? It must be!"

The impresario took the implement from Sebastian's hands and peered closely at it. "A key? Better than that. I've been on the windy side of the law enough to know a picklock! And this, the best I've ever seen. Handsome! It could open any door, gate, or padlock in Hamelin-Loring! Aha, my boy, your friend and your cat have given us our freedom."

"Presto, you're the gem of all cats," exclaimed Sebastian. "Duke of Gauli-Mauli? The Archduke! The Prince! No, the very King of Cats!"

Then he frowned and his face fell. "Even if this opens our cell—what then? We'll still be in the prison."

He took the key and looked at it with disappointment. In another moment he snapped his fingers and cried:

"Yes! I remember! The Chief Groom! Nicholas told me—Quicksilver, if we can reach the stables—"

"Chief Groom?" replied Quicksilver. "Stables? What's that to do with us? Do you mean to gallop on horseback out the palace gate?"

"Never mind for now," Sebastian answered, hurrying to the bars and slipping the key into the lock. He held his breath, terrified the lock would rasp. But it opened as smoothly as if it had been buttered. Heart pounding, he took Presto under his arm and beckoned Quicksilver to follow.

Near the end of the passage, the jailer snored in a chair, his feet on a wooden table. With Quicksilver treading stealthily behind him. Sebastian was about to make his way up the flight of steps beyond the jailer's post. He stopped short. Heaped on the floor, as though brought to add even more weight to his crime, were his bag and the rest of his belongings. Fallstick had been cheated of his prize. Sebastian's heart leaped when he saw the fiddle.

Quicksilver was urgently prodding him to move along. Sebastian hesitated. The violin—he could not force himself to leave it behind. Cautiously, he reached out and picked up the instrument and the bow. The strings thrilled and murmured in answer to his touch. The fiddle was his once more.

At the faint sound, however, the jailer wakened. His eyes popped at the sight of the two prisoners now suddenly at large. An instant later he was on his feet, shouting an alarm.

Quicksilver sprang past Sebastian and threw himself on the jailer. "Run for it, lad! I'll settle this one."

Presto jumped free of his master's hold and darted up the steps, with Sebastian racing after. At the head of the stairway, a hasty glance backward told Sebastian the impresario had stunned his opponent and was following. But the jailer's outcry had brought a company of guards on the double from the armory, forcing Sebastian to dodge around a corner before they could glimpse him.

He lost sight of Quicksilver. Presto was streaking ahead. Sebastian, to his dismay, realized his flight had brought him to the central hallways of the palace.

He pelted along an arcade, turned, then dashed through a long antechamber. A blaze of light dazzled him. He stopped, confused and half blinded.

Candles flamed in banks from an upper gallery and blazed in the crystals of chandeliers. Courtiers and their ladies in all their finery swirled across the gleaming floor. The bright music of an orchestra filled his ears. Sebastian cried out in despair. He had blundered into the Grand Ballroom of the Glorietta. There, enthroned on a low stage draped in crimson velvet, flanked by guards in full-dress uniforms, by robed councillors and liveried attendants, sat Count Grinssorg, Regent of Hamelin-Loring.

Sebastian stared. He had imagined a misshapen giant, an ogre, a monster more bloated than The Purse, more foppish than the barber. He saw a horror worse than any of these. In robes of high state, Grinssorg was a superbly handsome figure; but the jet-black hair set off features cold and rigid as marble, utterly unlined, smooth, unmarked by the faintest crease or furrow. Never in his life had Sebastian seen a face so untouched by human feeling or failing: bloodless lips which never could have laughed; iron eyes which never could have wept. The Regent's pitiless glance froze all it reached. Yet even as Sebastian tried to turn away, the eyes held him until he felt himself emptied, dwindled, reduced to nothing; no longer a man but a lifeless thing; less than any living creature, no more than a stick or stone.

He shrank back. As he did, a footman seized him by the collar and, glimpsing the fiddle, whispered furiously:

"Rogue! What are you about? You dare shirk a performance, you lazy lout! Back to the orchestra, where you belong! To your place again! This instant!"

With that, he gave the supposed court musician a shove that sent Sebastian into the ranks of the orchestra just beyond the overhanging gallery.

The musicians were too busy to heed one more fiddler. Seizing on this as his last and only hiding place and desperately hoping to go unnoticed, Sebastian tucked the fiddle under his chin, caught up the tune, and joined in playing for all he was worth.

The violin quickened into life. Its voice sang out, clear

and brilliant above all the orchestra, filling the ballroom and soaring to the highest vaults of the ceiling. The musicians halted, wonderstruck. Sebastian, sure he would be lost amid the orchestra, now found himself playing alone, with every eye upon him.

Grinssorg sprang from his throne as the guards burst into the ballroom. Ready to turn and run, Sebastian was rooted to the spot. Try as he would, he could not stop playing. The guards streamed toward him. Then, to his astonishment, only half-a-dozen paces away, they faltered and fell back. Sabers, pistols, and muskets dropped from their hands. Their mouths gaped and their eyes bulged in disbelief at their own behavior—for, in another moment, they began to dance.

The musicians themselves jumped from their chairs, flung aside their instruments, and followed the guards' example. The courtiers, even those crowding the farthest arcades, moved their feet in time to Sebastian's music. A company of dragoons, storming into the palace at the commotion, fell to dancing that same instant.

The sound of the violin overflowed the ballroom to reach every corner of the Glorietta. In the scullery, cooks and bakers, potboys and serving girls dropped spoons and ladles, kicked over kettles, and danced madly amid shattered crockery. Lackeys and court councillors, chambermaids and countesses, all trod their measures.

Except for Sebastian, whose playing had turned faster and wilder, there was no man or woman, noble or commoner in all the palace who had not broken into some kind of jig, reel, hornpipe, minuet, or waltz, whirling and spinning about in any way that struck their fancy.

Though he fought against it with all his will, even the

Regent was caught in the net of music. He had risen from his throne, rage swelled his face, but he could no more stop dancing than any in the Glorietta.

Sebastian's fingers sped as the violin willed. The outpouring notes overwhelmed him in golden waves; yet, plunging deeper and deeper into the music, he played on.

The dancers, one by one, fell exhausted. Grinssorg alone kept his feet. His eyes blazed; on his forehead rose a pulsing vein that writhed like a white serpent clinging to his brow. He had drawn his sword. Each step brought him closer to Sebastian.

The song of the violin had risen to unbearable beauty. In one clear moment, Sebastian knew as surely as if the carved features on the scroll had spoken, that each note was turning his heartbeats into melody; and at the end of it there could be only his death.

But the music, he realized with the same clarity, had become a fatal snare for the Regent. Grinssorg's body convulsed, his face twisted with hatred and agony. His life, too, was at the mercy of the fiddle.

Sebastian felt his strength failing, though he could neither drop the bow nor wrench the violin away. He hoped only to outlast the Regent. But, in the next instant, he saw that Grinssorg was no longer dancing.

Then Sebastian staggered under a sudden blow, toppled, and went spinning into a black pit of silence.

XXXIII ❦ How One Song Ended and Others Began

WHAT struck Sebastian with such force to knock him off his feet and send him headlong was the only one in all the Glorietta who had not been caught up in the music: Presto.

Separated from his master and anxiously seeking him, the white cat had made his way up a staircase into the gallery overlooking the orchestra. From there, Presto had launched himself in a powerful spring to land on his favorite perch: Sebastian's shoulder.

And so, when Sebastian, dazed and shaken, opened his eyes, the first thing he saw was Presto, nuzzling him with fond concern and purring like a beehive.

"Presto?" Sebastian murmured. "Did the music take your life along with mine?"

He put one hand to his whirling head and embraced the cat with the other. Little by little, his wits came back to him and he glanced around quickly. Throughout the Grand Ballroom the fallen dancers stirred and began climbing, bewildered, to their feet.

One did not rise: the Regent, stiff and motionless in the middle of the ballroom floor.

Sebastian tried to clamber up, only to drop back and cry out in anguish. Under the impact of Presto's leap, he had fallen forward, still holding the violin, which now lay beside him, broken past repair.

Dazed and grief-stricken, he clutched at the bits and pieces of the beautiful instrument. The carved head was split apart, the face shattered and disfigured; the body no more than matchwood. The neck had snapped in two, and the strings hung lifeless from the broken pegs of the fiddle, now forever silent.

At the far end of the ballroom, the portals burst open. Quicksilver was there. Nicholas and Benno hastened through the ranks of stunned guardsmen and dragoons. Isabel ran toward him and a moment later was in his arms.

In the chambers of the First Minister of State, the curtains had been drawn back and all the casements flung wide open to the sunlight. On the long council table, Presto sported among pens, papers, and inkwells, and the Great Seal of Hamelin-Loring itself, heedless of Sebastian's plea to behave with a little more dignity.

But the First Minister took the cat's exploring in good part, and laughed indulgently.

"Let him have his way," said Nicholas. "He saved your life, my friend, and for that I'll deny him nothing."

Though Nicholas wore the scarlet sash of his new office, his plump features still held his usual look of innocent astonishment at finding himself in such a place. He turned to Isabel.

"Now then, Princess, to affairs of state. Until the Grand Council's formed and the folk of Hamelin-Loring have their own voice, you shall have to speak for them. You've already done more in a fortnight than all your ancestors together. Has anything been overlooked?"

"We think not," replied Isabel. "Andreas and his fellows have found justice. The washerwoman, too. Count Lobelieze—The Purse—is hardly gratified at his exile, especially without his ill-gotten fortune; yet he prefers it to incarceration. That is—he'd rather be turned out of the realm than clapped into prison. Baron Purn-Hessel has consented to be Royal Treasurer; we're sure he'll serve us honestly and well. Flasch is pardoned, though more at your insistence than ours."

"And Quicksilver," Sebastian put in. "I think your favor pleased him best. The *Royal* Gaullimaufry-Theatricus! By Appointment to Her Highness—he's already got it painted all over his wagons."

"So be it, then," said Nicholas, "and matters are settled."

"Save one," Isabel answered, gently putting her hand on Sebastian's arm. "A stubborn fiddler who'll not allow us the pleasure of granting him even the rank of Chevalier."

Sebastian smiled ruefully and shook his head. "Alas, there's no rank or badge to make a better fiddler of me, without a fiddle."

"True enough," said Nicholas. "And yet—"

Next moment, Sebastian found himself holding a violin which Nicholas, like a conjurer, had put into his hands. The violin was as beautiful, in its own fashion, as Lelio's had been.

Nicholas laughed heartily at Sebastian's astonishment.

"Even the remarkable Captain had trouble finding one like this."

"My thanks to you!" Sebastian exclaimed in delight, as he turned the violin this way and that, the better to admire it.

"But Nicholas—I hope you won't tell me this, too, is accursed."

"Have no fear," Nicholas replied. "You can play to your heart's content, for there's not even a hint of that. If indeed your other fiddle ever was accursed."

"Yet it destroyed Grinssorg," Sebastian answered. "And if Presto hadn't jumped when he did, it would have been the end of me."

"A strange instrument, surely," replied Nicholas. "Accursed—we'll never know. Grinssorg? Did music triumph over inhumanity? And you—was the music taking your life? Or were you offering it to what you loved? Let's not try to guess, but only say: It happened thus, make of it what you will."

Sebastian nodded. "And I won't try to guess why the fiddle played for me at all. A true musician? Worthy of the instrument? I hope someday I will be. But one thing the fiddle taught me: before, music was my living; now, it's my life."

Benno, who had changed his beggar's rags for the attire of Lord Chamberlain, came to announce that the new cabinet councillors sought an audience with the First Minister.

Leaving Nicholas to his duties, Sebastian and Isabel made their way from the palace into the Royal Pleasure Gardens, following Presto, who frisked ahead after butterflies. There, by a stone balustrade, they watched the folk of Loringhold who had come to marvel at the parks, the fountains, and the flowered avenues.

By Isabel's decree, for the first time in the history of Hamelin-Loring, the gates of the Glorietta were open in welcome to all.

"And now, sir," Isabel declared with mock solemnity, "is this true, as you implied to our First Minister, that you'll keep at your music in all good earnest?"

"Why, so I shall, ma'am," Sebastian replied in the same tone. He grinned at her. "Lelio's fiddle made you laugh, very likely for the first time in your life, and I hope my new one does as well."

Isabel smiled. "Yes, you made us laugh for the first time. At least, out loud. Though we were close to it, when you said such impertinent things about our Councillors-Royal. But you made us furious, too. When you called us skinny and scrawny—"

"But that was the time you crowned me with a bucket of water—"

"Then when you called us Priss-and-Prim—"

"As I thought you were," Sebastian returned, "before you turned out to be such a splendid dancer in the Theatricus."

"We hope we turn out as good a Princess," answered Isabel. "We—no, it shall be 'we' no longer, but 'I.' Not even a Princess has the right to speak for all her subjects, that's for the Grand Council to do. But Nicholas tells me I must keep my throne and stay as long as I'm needed."

Children raced along the path near the balustrade. Sebastian and Isabel were silent then, watching them at their games.

ne!" cried one little girl. "I'm Princess Isabel, it's
n!"

o, it's mine," retorted another, and they began
uting and arguing the matter until one boy declared:

"Have done! You can't all be Princess Isabel at once!
I'll be Sebastian. He's going to marry the Princess, so I'm
the one to choose."

At this, they dashed off down the pathway, the girls
shrieking and giggling at the top of their voices, with the
self-styled Sebastian in hot pursuit, while Sebastian himself turned to Isabel.

"Is there truth in their game? Will a princess ever wed
a fiddler?"

"If he's won her heart," Isabel replied. "And so he has.
The heart of a princess never aches—as all the court
councillors told me. Even in that they were wrong. For
mine does. I'll be glad when I can give up my crown, and
the sooner the better. Until then—are you sure you'll
not change your mind and stay in the Glorietta?"

"A courtier?" cried Sebastian. "His Excellency the
Chevalier Fiddlesticks? The Most Honorable Squawk-
and-Scrape? Ah, no, before I marry a Princess I'll be a
noble among fiddlers, not a fiddler among nobles! The
music I heard—once, you said I should write it down.
And I will. Or try at least to learn. Quicksilver's off again
with the Royal Gallimaufry-Theatricus. If our paths
cross, he might be glad for a composer to set his plays to
music. And if Presto's to have his gold saucer and silk pillow, I'll earn them for him myself."

Presto, hearing his name, gave up his butterfly chase
and jumped onto Sebastian's shoulder. Isabel reached out
and gently stroked the cat.

"Duke of Gauli-Mauli," she murmured, "I thi
master's as much a scamp as you. Nevertheless,
Duke, you're charged with a royal command and
mission: to keep good watch on my fiddler."

On the day Sebastian said his fondest farewells to Isabel
and Nicholas, the streets of Loringhold were bursting
with men, women, and children laughing, singing, dancing, their faces happier than he had ever seen them; for
the Grand Council had been called to its first meeting.
With Presto on his shoulder, he started through the
crowd. Lingering a moment, he turned back for a last
sight of the Glorietta.

As he did, a ragged street singer, seeing he carried a
fiddle in the bag under his arm, called out to him:

"Hold a moment! Since we're both in the same trade,
hear a song from me. For no more than a penny! The
newest in Hamelin-Loring! All about a fellow named Sebastian: 'How Sebastian Flew on a Fiddlestick!' 'How Sebastian Sailed to the Moon'—"

"Merry tunes, surely," replied Sebastian. "But have
you none that say whether this fellow Sebastian was a
good fiddler?"

The street singer threw back his head and laughed.
"What's that to do with anything? A good fiddler?
There's no merriment in that. If you think so, you've
much to learn. I took you for a colleague, but I see now
you're only an apprentice!"

At this, Sebastian himself began to laugh. "Why, so I
am, friend! Indeed, so I am!"

And he set off on his way again.